GILLIAM COUNTY PUBLIC LIBRARY
134 SOUTH MAIN STREET
PO BOX 34
CONDON, OREGON 97823

DATE DUE

ACROSS THE RÍO BRAVO

Center Point
Large Print

Also by R.W. Stone and available from
Center Point Large Print:

Badman's Pass

**This Large Print Book carries the
Seal of Approval of N.A.V.H.**

ACROSS THE RÍO BRAVO

R. W. Stone

CENTER POINT LARGE PRINT
THORNDIKE, MAINE

This Circle Ⓥ Western is published by
Center Point Large Print in the year 2017 in
co-operation with Golden West Literary Agency.

First Edition
July, 2017

Printed in the United States of America
on permanent paper.
Set in 16-point Times New Roman type.

ISBN: 978-1-68324-452-3

Library of Congress Cataloging-in-Publication Data

Names: Stone, R. W., author.
Title: Across the Río Bravo : a Circle V western / R. W. Stone.
Description: First edition. | Thorndike, Maine : Center Point Large Print, 2017.
Identifiers: LCCN 2017011288 | ISBN 9781683244523
    (hardcover : alk. paper)
Subjects: LCSH: Large type books. | GSAFD: Western stories.
Classification: LCC PS3619.T67 A65 2017 | DDC 813/.6—dc23
LC record available at https://lccn.loc.gov/2017011288

DEDICATION:

This one is for Dr. Zack Morgan
one of the finest men and closest friends
I've ever known.

Nothing in the world can take the place of persistence.

—Calvin Coolidge

Preface

In 1870 a boundary treaty was signed between the United States of America and *Los Estados Unidos de Méjeco*. This treaty was intended to settle all disputes relating to the Río Grande, or as it is known south of the border, *El Río Bravo del Norte.*

The Native American tribes who had lived in the area for generations before a white man ever arrived there were not invited to participate in the negotiations, were not included in the final decision, or even remotely considered in the treaty.

The border between Mexico and the United States now runs from Imperial Beach, California in the west, to Brownsville, Texas in the east. The present-day border serpentines its way along a designated course right through the middle of the river at its deepest channel.

Geographically the Río Bravo flows through the state of Texas, which borders four Mexican states—Tamaulipas, Nuevo León, Coahuila, and Chihuahua. New Mexico borders two Mexican states, Chihuahua and Sonora, while Arizona borders Sonora and Baja California. The state of California borders only Baja California to its south.

Regardless of any of the imaginary lines drawn on a map, the Río Grande is one of the most historically significant waterways in the world. It has been depicted one way or another in countless books and movies. It even has a John Ford/John Wayne movie named after it. To Western aficionados it is almost as if the river has a personality of its own.

Proudly, by the turn of the 20th Century, the United States of America had not been invaded for a hundred years. Not since the War of 1812 had her borders ever been violated. On March 9, 1916, however, a Mexican revolutionary led remnants of an army called *La Division del Norte* on a raid across the border into the small American town of Columbus, New Mexico. They attacked the nearby fort, stole horses and supplies, burned part of the town, and ultimately killed nineteen people before fleeing south, back across the border.

The raid was seen as an affront to American sovereignty, one that at the time the American federal government refused to tolerate. A mighty army was assembled, and one of the true heroes of the Spanish-American War, John J. Pershing, now a brigadier general, was appointed to head a great expedition.

This general was tasked with following the *Division del Norte* into Mexico, destroying it, and capturing or killing its leader. There was no doubting the orders given to General Pershing. He was to teach the Mexican leader and any other rebel who dared violate U.S. territory a swift lesson in American politics.

Prologue

An early morning mist hung in the air surrounding the peaceful town. Hidden within the fog were over a hundred bloodthirsty men who comprised the makeshift army that was preparing to attack.

The men thought of themselves as *revolucionarios*, soldiers of the Mexican revolution. They followed an inspirational leader that they all believed was a hero, one who, it was hoped, would someday become the savior of their nation. In truth, their general, while certainly brave enough, was an unscrupulous, egotistical fanatic. Although he portrayed himself as a humble and patriotic man, he was, deep down, personally ambitious to a fault and capable of coldly calculated and horrific acts of unspeakably barbaric cruelty.

This army followed their leader, a man who, although born a farmer, had gone into banditry by his sixteenth birthday. The man claimed he was forced to do so to hide from corrupt authorities. The real reason though was that he had shot a rancher who supposedly accosted one of his sisters.

His skills as a fugitive bandit, his fighting ability, and his knowledge of the land later allowed him to achieve great success as a rebel fighter in the uprising against the president of Mexico. He eventually rose in stature sufficiently enough to command an army of rebels that at one point numbered in the thousands.

Such leaders are often desirable in the fury of battle, but when political tides change and peace becomes more attractive, their warrior skills are later perceived as a threat to the very same group that had loyally supported them.

Such had been the fate of this general and sadly his last battle had been a disaster. With fewer troops now and with his former supporters turning against him, he had decided to seek a quick and easy victory for his diminishing army.

It mattered little to him that he was attacking a town of innocent men, women, and children. It mattered little that the attack would be unprovoked, without warning, and engaged primarily against civilians. And it mattered even less that he was attacking a town on foreign soil.

The general had divided his troops into a two-pronged attack by well over a hundred men against a small American town that had absolutely nothing to do with his revolution. The soldiers had been briefed very little, but it wouldn't have mattered how much they had been briefed. The average revolutionary cared very little about anything except the final outcome of the cause, while the rest of the soldiers cared only about survival and personal comfort.

As far as most of the men were concerned, the end justified the means. Besides, who cared what happened to a town full of *gringos*?

The town below was asleep as the rebel army poised for the attack. Machetes had been sharpened, guns had been cleaned and oiled, and rifles were loaded. Little did anyone know it at the time but this was to be a defining moment in history.

The sleepy town was Columbus, New Mexico and the people living there were about to be attacked by an invading army from across the border. An army led by General Pancho Villa.

Chapter One

The old trooper sat astride a large black stallion perched atop a high grassy knoll. He had left his ranch and come up to this nearby place to ponder things. Here it was quiet. Here it was shady, and the view of the surrounding area was magnificent. It was a calm and peaceful place. It was a good spot to relax and contemplate the future.

The man puffed on a well-worn, full-bent, hand-carved, briar wood pipe. It had seen so much use it now seemed almost a part of him.

Looking out over the landscape, there was one thing that kept returning to his thoughts. It was the same question many have asked of themselves at such an age: *How the Sam Hill did I ever get to this point in my life?* To the old man, it seemed like it was just yesterday when he had stood, ramrod straight, on that distant Cuban battlefield. Through the smoke that wafted up from his pipe, he could almost visualize his Army unit's flags billowing. When the wind blew across the knoll, it made the tree leaves rustle and that somehow reminded him of the music from the military band that had played on the parade ground back on that glorious day.

Even after all this time the words of the commanding officer of his regiment still resonated in his mind: *For conspicuous gallantry, above and beyond the call of duty, it is my honor and privilege to award to Sergeant Major Thaddeus McCallum this medal. . . .*

A tear began to form in the corner of the old man's eye as he recalled his comrades from the old unit cheering: *Hip, hip, hurrah! Hurray for Thad McCallum, the Iron Sergeant!*

That of course had been back in 1898 when the Spanish-American War had finally come to an end. Even though handing out medals had been the order of the day, there was just cause for Sergeant Thad McCallum to take pride in his.

McCallum had more than earned his honors in battle, but by the time his tour of duty was over, he couldn't help but wonder what the future would hold in store for an ex-soldier. Back then the forty-five-year-old had known little else of life other than a twenty-five-year hitch in the military.

Long ago, traits such as gallantry and camaraderie were things to be admired, but almost eighteen years had come and gone since that day on the field of valor. As far as McCallum was concerned, it seemed that these days the country had all but turned its back on such patriotic ideals.

The old trooper recalled the last tavern he'd been in. A sign in the window had proclaimed:

No dogs, coloreds, or soldiers allowed. He had shaken his head when he read the sign, noting sadly that the Army hadn't even made the top of the list.

As for the others, hell, as far as he was concerned it had been Lieutenant Black Jack Pershing's 10th Cavalry's "colored" buffalo soldiers who had taken the brunt of the fire on San Juan Hill during the war.

Of course, there was never a doubt in his mind that Colonel Teddy was a true hero and as brave as they come, but the truth was his Rough Riders were white and were therefore more "colorful" to the newspapers than the Negro soldiers. McCallum realized there was no way those black troopers would ever be recognized by the press for their truly heroic fight. But he and the other soldiers who fought there knew what had happened.

Crawling up Kettle Hill with Roosevelt was certainly hell on earth, but once they reached the summit, the Rough Riders could clearly see that the soldiers of the 10th who were assaulting San Juan were facing even worse counter-fire. That didn't stop the Buffalo Soldiers, though. They climbed straight up, right through Spanish Mauser rifles and German-built, rapid-fire guns as if being propelled from behind by an unstoppable force.

Their attack was so inspiring, the Rough

Riders turned their own machine-guns back on the Spanish and then charged off Kettle Hill and over toward San Juan Hill to help win the day. Those who remained standing at the end of the fight didn't feel much like cheering. At the time, it didn't even feel much like anyone had truly won. Far too many of their troopers were on the ground, dead, and the only color that mattered that day was blood red.

The big black horse shook his head and snorted, snapping the old man out of his reverie. He sighed, and then rapped the bottom of his pipe against the palm of his left hand. Turning the pipe over, he emptied the dottle from its bowl. He slowly placed the briar pipe back in the soft deerskin tobacco pouch he always carried, and then returned the pouch to his coat pocket.

"What to do, boy? That's the question." He was speaking to his horse, but clearly the words were meant for himself. In another pocket, there was a letter that had recently arrived for him at the post office back in town.

This far out in the western countryside such things as telephones and postal couriers who made deliveries riding those new-fangled motor carriages were still considered rarities. The letter in question contained a rather difficult request from Albert Shaw, an old friend from way back when. McCallum had served with Al for many years until an accidental discharge from an inexperienced recruit's rifle crippled Shaw's left leg. The corporal had been a true friend and on more than one occasion had pulled Thad's fat from the fryer.

McCallum took out a pair of spectacles and put them on with a frown. Although he could still see long distances practically as well as an Apache, for some reason he now had problems focusing on objects that were close. Being far-sighted they called it. He detested having to wear these glasses that were a constant reminder of his age. Besides, they pinched his nose and ears.

Thad unfolded the letter and read it again:

I sent our boy Jeff to learn the photography trade from my brother who lives in Columbus, New Mexico. The problem now is that my wife Margaret has taken seriously ill and the doctors aren't giving her much hope for the long term. I'd like Jeff to come home to be with his mother, but despite two letters and a telegraph I haven't had a single reply from him.

I know it is a lot to ask of you but since you live in the same state as my brother Jacob, I thought perhaps you might travel down to Columbus and locate Jeff for us.

Understand, I normally would not impose on our friendship in such an unreasonable manner, but I simply cannot leave Maggie alone under the circumstances.

We both are becoming very concerned about the lad. Although Jeff is rather inexperienced about some things, he is good and honest and I can't imagine him ignoring our pleas. Especially not where his mother is concerned.

"Damn," McCallum muttered. He wiped his brow. "Not Maggie."

Thad McCallum had been best man at their wedding and had never seen a more beautiful bride. Hell, if she hadn't been so in love with Al, he might have asked her himself. Thad smiled sadly at the thought.

Marriage hadn't been in the books for the old soldier. Too many different posts, too much time in the field, and too little money saved to offer a decent woman any hope for a happy life together.

Oh, there had been opportunities, especially for a tall and good-looking young man, but nothing ever worked out. Right man, wrong woman, or wrong man, right woman. Who knew? As he remembered her, Maggie was as good a prospect as he'd ever met, but she had taken one look at Corporal Shaw and fallen head over heels in love. Maybe it was just as well, Thad reflected with a shrug.

McCallum slowly refolded the letter and put it back in his pocket. He did the same with his glasses, and then rubbed the bridge of his nose.

Thad finally collected his reins. "Guess it's time for you and me to take a little trip," he said, nudging the black gently with his right spur. "So, we might as well get on with it, boy."

Chapter Two

Pedro Peralta nodded his head while he listened to his *jefe*, the Spanish word for "boss" that Pedro always used. To be completely honest, McCallum never fancied himself as Peralta's boss and he certainly didn't treat Pedro like an employee. He had been together with Thad on their ranch for almost eight years now and had helped rebuild the place after McCallum had purchased it.

Pedro had grown to be as much a part of the ranch as Thad. He was a friend, confidant, and colleague, but try as he might, McCallum couldn't get Pedro to stop calling him *jefe*.

After retiring from military service, Thad had wandered for a time trying to find just the right job for his own future. He had enough retirement pay to last him for a while, but not enough for the long term. The government had never been particularly generous about such things.

McCallum knew there was no way he was going to punch cows for the rest of his life and the thought of clerking or banking gave him dyspepsia. He finally ended up in front of a Pinkerton agency in Denver, Colorado where the idea of having some freedom of movement with a sense of public service appealed to him.

The possibility of a little adventure now and then didn't hurt much, either.

For ten years, the detective job took him all over the Southwest. While much of it was investigative, some was undercover work, and there was also a fair share of tracking down wanted criminals. The adventure part certainly hadn't disappointed him, especially if you defined an adventure as moments of excitement and terror, during which time you wished it wasn't happening to you.

McCallum thrived in the game and sincerely appreciated the commendations he occasionally received from his two bosses, Robert and William Pinkerton. The founder, Allan Pinkerton, had left both sons in control of the agency.

His past cavalry training had made McCallum well suited for the agency's paramilitary duties, especially for the field work in which he excelled. Ever since the Pinkertons had first caught the government's fancy, there was no shortage of city types who would work for them, investigating con artists, blackmailers, and petty thieves.

The problem however, was that on more than one occasion the agency had to pursue leads into the rougher outlands, and it was in the back country that McCallum had originally honed his skills. Eventually he ended up in charge of the whole Southwest division and in turn received a substantial salary for his duties.

About ten years into the job the great-grandson of Allan Pinkerton took over the company. Like any bureaucracy with a new boss there is always a flexing of muscle and a desire to innovate. Younger men were envious of the older division chief and it wasn't long before McCallum got fed up with responding to constant memos, criticisms, and ridiculous instructions from the higher-ups who simply wanted to try something new or different, even if it made no sense whatsoever.

It didn't matter much that he had been, and technically still was, one of their most successful agents. Under such circumstances there is always a "what-have-you-done-lately?" attitude, so it wasn't very long after the new management took over that the disgruntled detective began to look around for a change of scenery.

That decision eventually took him south to a small ranch north of Deming, New Mexico. At the time, Deming was a relatively new town and McCallum reasoned that with the growth of any settlement the need for supplies and livestock would also increase.

There was no way a man like Thaddeus McCallum would ever end up running a general store, but if he had learned anything during his years in the cavalry it was horses. He decided that it made sense to start breeding, training, and selling them. He hoped it would make for a nice living.

Pedro Peralta in his younger days had been what Northerners call a "peeler" and there was none better. A peeler is a specialist in breaking wild horses and retraining them into riding horses. Some peelers still favored the traditionally harsh techniques such as throwing the horse to the ground and hog-tying it to break its spirit, but not Pedro.

Instead, Peralta would construct a circular ring that he used for the horses he trained. He would walk the horses all day long inside the pen, constantly changing directions, and he talked to the horses until a bond was established. Sooner than anyone would ever believe possible, even the wildest of broncos would end up following him around like a big puppy. From that point on it was a relatively simple procedure for Pedro to teach them to accept both saddle and bridle.

Their ranch was never very large but it was profitable and the two men made a very good living. Thad would often ride out for weeks at a time on buying expeditions while Pedro tended to the ranch's chores and supervised the other wranglers they had hired.

Eight years had passed and McCallum never regretted his decision. He was sure his friend Pedro hadn't either. They had originally met when McCallum first rode into Deming to inquire about the small outlying ranch he had passed on the trail. It seemed abandoned and Thad figured, if it were for sale, it would serve his intended purpose.

During the ride into town his horse had begun to act up, but, although he checked him over, Thad couldn't seem to identify the problem. When he finally rode up to the local bank, he couldn't help but notice a middle-aged Mexican sitting on a bench over on the boardwalk, whittling a small stick.

Peralta had been a slender man, sporting a black mustache that protruded out from under a rather large, round, and embroidered sombrero that was typical of the *vaqueros*.

While he was dismounting, Thad's horse began to shy again and started to whinny. Normally that horse was a very steady mount, so once on the ground McCallum ran his hands along the horse's legs, checked the hoofs, and even opened his mouth.

Frustrated that he could find no obvious cause for the problem, Thad muttered to himself and left the animal tied to the hitching post while he entered the bank. Half an hour later Thad had a fairly good history of the town and the ranch in question. He knew he would be able to afford it if he decided to settle there.

His intention was to survey the town and get a feel for the local inhabitants, but as soon as he began to mount, his horse began to buck and whinny again.

"What the hell?" he asked himself, disturbed. Thad dismounted and stood there, looking at the horse, his hand stroking his chin in puzzled thought. "What's got into you, boy?" he said aloud.

Without a word the Mexican *vaquero* got up, strode past him, and approached the horse. He put a gentle hand on Thad's shoulder when he passed him as if to say: "Please, just get out of the way."

The manner in which he did it sparked no hostility, but it did cause a great deal of surprise on McCallum's part. He was a tall, strong man and straight of stature. He was an ex-sergeant and an ex-agency division boss. Being told to move out of the way was something Thaddeus McCallum was simply not accustomed to.

Peralta walked up to the horse, rubbed a gentle hand along the big animal's neck, and then began removing its tack.

"Hey, now, wait a minute!" Thad protested.

The Mexican put up his right arm, signaling for McCallum to keep back, all the while petting the horse with his other hand.

"*Un momento, señor*. Please," the *vaquero* said.

McCallum took a step back and watched the man with growing curiosity.

The *vaquero* worked his way back over the horse slowly, removing both the saddle and blanket. He carried them over to the boardwalk and flipped them over. He then stooped down by the saddle to inspect it, and after a moment he smiled. With a flick of his fingers he asked McCallum to come over.

"See here, *señor*?" he asked. "Right here?"

Thad McCallum took a close look, trying to determine what was wrong with the underside of his saddle. He ran his hand through the fleece lining on the saddle bottom and suddenly retracted it in pain. "Ouch! Damn it!" he cried.

Pedro began shaking the blanket and checking it over as well.

"These little things, they pinch the horse. That is why he give you the trouble, *señor*," he explained. "There were some sand spurs nestled deep in the wool lining. These burs are small but they are a particularly nasty prickly part of certain weeds. Their thorns pinch whoever or whatever they brush up against and stick and sting like the devil."

"Well I'll be a monkey's uncle," McCallum said, laughing. He extended a hand. Pedro took it, and they shook. The Mexican was somewhat embarrassed by McCallum's exuberant thanks, and became even more so when Thad invited him to have a drink in the local tavern. He couldn't help but consent. Thaddeus McCallum had always been a hard man to refuse.

Once inside the bar, a place aptly called The Watering Hole, the two men walked up to the bar. "Bartender, two beers please. Big and cold," McCallum said.

The barman, a rotund and balding man wearing a dirty apron, seemed rather uncomfortable, as if he was put out for some reason. But, after a small shrug, he served them. Thad raised his beer and thanked Pedro once again.

"Should have figured that one out," he said, referring to his horse. "I must have picked those burs up while camping out on the trail. Probably tossed the saddle down on a bush full of 'em. I'm usually more careful about such things."

Pedro nodded. He believed the tall Yankee. "That blanket you use, she is still pretty good, but the cinch needs replacing," he remarked. "It is . . . how you say . . . frayed. It, too, is rubbing your horse underneath."

There is an old saying that goes to the effect that when things seem the most pleasant, life decides to crap on you. McCallum and Peralta had found kindred spirits. The two men both appreciated horses and tended to judge men by performance, not appearance.

They were halfway into enjoying their beers when two drovers got up from their table and butted up to the bar right next to them. The larger of the two men gave Pedro a dirty look, and then turned to face McCallum.

"We don't cotton to sharing our drinks with no greaser," he said. The other drover laughed loudly. They both wore long wide chaps and carried their revolvers in low-hanging holsters, Texas style.

Thad readjusted himself so that his back was square to the bar, his beer mug held tightly in his left hand, waist high. He nodded his head in the direction of the barman.

"Greaser? Not sure I catch your drift. This bartender seems nice and clean, except maybe for his apron. His complexion seems fine to me. Now, I know for a fact that my friend here uses hair tonic, not grease, so just who the hell are you referring to? Me, perhaps? You think I'm greasy?"

Pedro just stood there, shocked.

The drover, who couldn't have been more than twenty-five, looked the stranger up and down, appraising him. What he thought he saw was just another grizzled old man. Judging by his response, maybe he was even a little touched.

True, the gent did carry a Colt Single Action revolver that was often referred to as a Peacemaker, but those days out West almost everyone carried a sidearm, so he didn't put much stock in it.

What the cowpoke failed to notice, however, was that the holster, although admittedly fairly worn, was exceptionally clean and well oiled. He also didn't stop to consider that the wood grip on the man's Colt—while not as fancy or engraved as the pistol Colonel Roosevelt had used going up San Juan Hill—was worn to a shine with years of constant use. A smarter or more experienced man would have known that wood doesn't get like that unless it has been handled countless times.

"You didn't answer my question, sonny. You saying I'm greasy?" Thad asked angrily.

The question took the drover a mite by surprise, but when he realized he was being ridiculed, it quickly got his dander up.

"If you are with that one, you are," the young drover replied rudely, nodding his head in the direction of Peralta.

"Because you are young, stupid, and a bigot, and because it is obvious to me you were raised improperly, I will give you one chance," Thad growled. "But only one, mind you. Back on out of here and get lost, and no harm will come to you."

Out of the corner of his eye McCallum took note of the second drover's position. Pedro hadn't moved and was standing as still as a statue. His arms were crossed in front of him and he was totally silent.

McCallum didn't have a clue as to whether he could count on any kind of help from Pedro. Thad remembered an adage he favored: *When in doubt rely on yourself first and yourself second.*

"Why, you feeble old man," the cowpuncher said, "who the hell do you think you are giving orders to anyway? You who don't even act like no decent white man." With that he went for his gun.

McCallum simply extended his left arm and then brought it down hard. He was still grasping the beer mug tightly when he did so. Just as the cowboy was pulling his gun upward out of his holster, the thick beer glass smacked the drover's gun hand right on top, behind the knuckles.

There are enough small bones and pressure points in the center of the top of the human hand that it doesn't take much to cause severe pain when it's hit just right. The pain can be excruciating.

The cowboy winced, fumbled his revolver, and finally dropped it. When he glanced up, he was staring at the business end of a Colt .45. In fact, he was more than staring. The gun in the older man's right hand was pressed dead center between his eyes.

Looking to his side, McCallum saw that Pedro had finally uncrossed his arms and was now pinning the second drover against the bar by the neck. Peralta's right arm was clutching a rather large machete that just moments before had been hanging unobtrusively from the left side of his belt.

"Back up!" McCallum ordered. He pressed the

pistol even harder against the drover's forehead. The man began walking backward, very slowly, one step at a time. Pedro Peralta followed Thad's lead, putting pressure on the machete lodged across the neck of the other drover as he, too, began walking toward the door.

Once McCallum exited the tavern and reached the end of the boarded sidewalk, he paused. His Colt remained tight against the man's head. He slowly pressed harder and harder. The drover, who at this point was more terrified than ever before in his life, began to arch his body backward, trying to get away from the business end of the pistol's barrel.

When McCallum decided the cowpoke had learned his lesson, he simply pressed the pistol barrel forward with force and the cowboy, now both scared and off balance, lost his footing and fell backward off the boardwalk, landing, hard, on his back in the dusty street.

Thad turned to watch the *vaquero* wave his big machete in the air, instructing the other drover to pick up his friend and leave.

"Guess we should finish that beer now, don't you think?" McCallum said with a smirk. "Then perhaps we should talk about ranching some horses."

Since that day, Pedro Peralta had been his constant companion. McCallum eventually bought the ranch and together over the years they had built it up into a very profitable enterprise. They became successful quickly and the Rough Rider Ranch, as it was called, was currently doing a steady business in breeding, breaking, trading, and selling both draft and riding horses throughout the state.

Now, as they sat eating dinner, McCallum said: "Pedro, I'm gonna be taking a little trip down to the border area so I'm gonna need you to see to things while I'm gone."

"Haven't I always?" Pedro replied. "You going to buy more stock? We're pretty full up now as it is."

McCallum took a sip of coffee and shook his head. "Nope. This time I'm doing a favor for an old friend. Seems his son's done gone and got himself misplaced somewhere around Columbus. My friend wants me to ride down and check on the lad to see if he's all right. It's probably nothing, but I'm obligated. I have to go."

"Obligated, *jefe*?"

McCallum thought back to a stinking jungle on the way to Santiago, Cuba. In 1898 the First United States Volunteers were known as Wood's Weary Walkers, named after Colonel Leonard Wood, the unit's first commander. When Wood was promoted to overall command, his second in command, Colonel Theodore Roosevelt, took over the brigade. The volunteers later began calling themselves Roosevelt's Rough Riders, a name that finally stuck with them for good.

Recently promoted Brigadier General Leonard Wood was studying a map that had been stretched open over the lowered tailgate of a supply wagon when a corporal appeared with a message from Colonel Roosevelt.

"Corporal Shaw reportin' with a dispatch from Colonel Teddy," he said.

Always a stickler for rules, General Wood looked over his shoulder at the soldier with a stern expression on his face. "You mean Colonel Roosevelt, don't you, Corporal?"

"Yes, sir. Begging the general's pardon. Colonel Roosevelt s-sent this for you," Shaw stammered, handing over a crumpled envelope. He then politely took several rather exaggerated steps back and promptly bumped into his old friend, Sergeant Thaddeus McCallum.

"Ouch! Say, watch whose foot you're stepping on, you clumsy fool."

Shaw looked back and grinned. "Hard not to step on those big clodhoppers of yours. They're always in the way. So, Thaddeus, how ya been?"

McCallum spit off to his left and grinned. "Oh, you know, breathing in and out. Can't complain."

Shaw nodded his head. "You could, but you wouldn't. Leastwise not in front of the general."

"So, what's up with the dispatch?" Thad asked.

"Oh, Colonel Teddy's gone and got himself in

another fix, I reckon. Seems like after the Hill them Spaniards would have up and quit, but they's just fallin' back and snipin' at us. Like a dog nippin' your heels, I guess. The colonel wanted to try and circle around 'em, but went and got caught himself. Now he needs some back-up."

"Must be tough," McCallum replied.

"Colonel Teddy would have gone and done it all by his lonesome if he thought he had half a chance." Both men laughed.

"Hey, you two, cut the chit-chat and come over here," General Wood commanded. He pointed out a spot on his map. "Look here. I need you two to break through to Colonel Roosevelt's unit . . . here . . . and bring him this message." He paused to look up at both men.

"Sergeant McCallum, I'm sending you along so that when Corporal Shaw trips and shoots himself in the foot, you can carry the message on the rest of the way. It has to get through or we may lose a lot of very good men."

The two men looked at each other and grinned.

"Begging your pardon, sir, but when he does, is it all right with the general if I put the corporal out of his misery before I move on with the message?" McCallum joked.

General Wood grinned back. "Sure. Just see to it that the message gets through or I'll put *you* out of your misery. Understood?"

Both men snapped to attention and replied: "Yes, sir!"

An hour later the two men took off from the camp at a run. They were traveling light, having opted to leave their rifles back in camp to lessen the load. They both knew that if they did run into the enemy, two rifles wouldn't change the outcome much, especially in thick jungle brush. Instead, they chose to take extra canteens. Water in the Cuban heat was often more important than bullets.

After two and a half hours of running, they stopped for a short five-minute rest.

"You sure we shouldn't have brung them rifles with us?" Corporal Shaw asked. "What if we get there and there is a full-fledged battle. What then?"

Sergeant McCallum thought a moment. "If there is a big fight, then I'm sure there will be plenty of rifles on the ground we can pick up and use."

Al Shaw nodded his head glumly. "Guess you're right. Ready to go, Sarge?"

McCallum took a small swig from his canteen, replaced the cap, and nodded. "Last one there's an old Marine."

Almost an hour later they were slowly working their way through some heavy brush when McCallum stepped near the tangled base of a large mangrove tree. "Dammit, that hurt."

Corporal Shaw pulled his machete from its sheath and chopped the head off a large thin snake. "Cuban racer," he announced grimly.

"They're poisonous, aren't they?" Thad asked. He already knew the answer.

"Yep, but at least there's good news and bad news."

"What's the good news?" the sergeant asked.

"They are poisonous but they usually don't kill people your size."

"So, what's the bad news?" McCallum asked. He was worried.

"Well, out here in the jungle gettin' real sick is the same as bein' dead. That leg of yours is goin' to get big and sore mighty fast. You won't be able to travel far unless we do something real quick about that venom."

McCallum knew what would come next. "Well, just leave me and go on. You got to get that message to the colonel."

After forcing McCallum to sit down, Corporal Shaw took out a small pocket knife and cut open Thad's pant leg to expose the bite. It was already beginning to swell. He then struck a match and began to heat the knife's blade over the fire.

"Any chance it was a dry strike?" McCallum asked. Sometimes, when a snake bites, the venom fails to be injected into the victim.

Shaw shook his head. "Not judgin' by the swellin' and discoloration, Sarge. No way."

"Well, what the hell you waiting for? You're burning daylight."

Corporal Shaw looked up at the jungle foliage overhead. "Not much of that here, now, is there? Say, you want a swig of whiskey before I cut?"

Thad looked up eagerly. "You brought some?"

Corporal Shaw shook his head. "Nah. Just wonderin' is all."

"Asshole!" McCallum groaned as Shaw began to cut into the leg. Then Shaw bent over and began to suck whatever poison he could out through the cut.

"Just get this straight, Sarge. This don't make us no god-damned blood brothers or anything of the sort," Shaw stated, after spitting out the venom.

"You go to hell!" McCallum grunted.

The corporal next took a shell from his cartridge belt and, using the side of his pocket knife's blade, pried the bullet off the casing.

"What's that for?" Thad was almost afraid to ask.

"Read once where the Vikings used to cauterize bad wounds with heated swords. This'll be quicker." He then handed McCallum a small stick. "Here, you're probably gonna need it. Put this in your mouth and clamp down. It'll help you with the pain and keep you from bitin' your tongue." As an afterthought, he added: "Might keep you quiet, too."

"Asshole," Thad repeated as he placed the stick between his teeth and bit down.

Before the sergeant could react, Shaw emptied the gunpowder from the shell into the wound. McCallum grimaced but it was nothing like the pain that followed when the corporal struck a match and ignited the powder that was in the wound. "There, that should be good and cauterized."

"Oh, you lousy son-of-a-bitch," McCallum muttered just before passing out.

When he came to, it took a few seconds before he knew where he was. He finally realized that Corporal Shaw was carrying him through the jungle on his back.

Thad managed to look down and he saw that his leg had been wrapped in a field dressing. He figured he must have been out for an hour at the very least.

"Leave me here, Al," Thad urged. "We both can't make it and that message must get through."

"We'll get through, all right. I figure it can't be too far now, so stop tryin' to play the hero again. Besides, think of all the glory. I can see the headlines now. The Iron Sergeant delivers crucial dispatch on one leg with unknown corporal along merely for company."

"Screw you. Now leave me here and go on alone."

"Whose gonna make me? You gonna pull rank on me?" Al laughed.

Thad groaned. "Yeah, Corporal, that's an order."

"All right, Sergeant, fine. As soon as we get where we're goin', you can put me in for a court martial."

"Al, cut the bullshit. You know how important that dispatch is. Our boys' lives might be depending on it. Leave me. The orders were to get there as fast as we can."

Al Shaw nodded. "And that's exactly what we're doin'. We're goin' as fast as we can. Now shut up. All your yammerin' is makin' this harder. Ever think of eatin' less?"

Fortunately, the gods of war were on their side, and after one more day and a half the two men collapsed into the Rough Riders' lines. They were out of food and down to a few drops of water in their canteens.

"Sergeant McCallum has a dispatch for Colonel Teddy," Shaw said, glancing over at his friend. Thad was slumped on the ground. "After you wake him up, that is."

Corporal Shaw did receive a minor commendation later, but by that time the Iron Sergeant's fame had grown such that everyone simply took Al Shaw's word that the brigade owed everything to Sergeant McCallum. It only served to add to his already growing legend.

Obliged? Of course, he was. Thad owed the man his life.

"Whatcha bet you gonna find your friend's boy shacked up with a young *señorita*?" Pedro joked across the dinner table.

McCallum shook out the cobwebs from the past and considered that for a moment. "Won't say it ain't possible, but from what my friend tells me, this here's a good kid. Doesn't seem the kind to just up and disappear. Anyway, I'll find out soon enough."

"You gonna take the black?" Pedro asked, referring to McCallum's favorite horse.

"More than likely, but I'll probably travel part of the way with him on the train. These old bones don't like saddle-back riding all day as much as they used to. No sense pushing it when I don't have to."

Pedro nodded at him. He knew perfectly well the *jefe* was more than capable of riding just as far and as well as he ever had, but he also knew that as of late his friend had been complaining of rheumatism.

Peralta was a bit younger, but even he was beginning to have good days and bad days when it came to his joints. Especially first thing in the morning or when the weather suddenly turned cold.

"I'll make sure they double check his hoofs and I'll have your pack made up."

McCallum smiled. "Don't be such a damned mother hen. You know, you worry way too much, Pedro."

"And don't you forget to oil your Winchester if you are taking it along, *jefe*," Pedro reminded.

"Now I know you're getting addle-brained. When did I ever forget that?" McCallum joked.

When the U.S. Army went to war with Cuba, they generally carried either Springfield .45-70 single-action trap-door rifles or the newer .30-40 Krag side-loading, bolt-action rifles and carbines.

At heart, Colonel Theodore Roosevelt was a Winchester man and carried a model 1895 into battle instead of the Krag. In fact, he liked it so much he ordered another hundred and handed them out among his troops. The Winchester '95 was a John Browning design that could handle unbelievable breech pressures without a hitch. Thaddeus McCallum hadn't been separated from his since the day he first received it.

Chapter Three

The following morning Thad McCallum awoke early and checked his personal supplies. He buckled on his holster, pulled out the Colt Single Action, and checked the cylinder. Out of habit he always carried five rounds instead of six, making sure that the chamber directly under the firing pin was empty. It was a common practice that prevented accidental discharges should the pistol ever be dropped on its hammer. After replacing the pistol, he put on his overcoat and patted the side pocket, checking for his pipe and tobacco pouch.

McCallum looked around and scooped up a small bag of licorice treats that was on a table near the door. He then put the bag in his other pocket.

Thad had started chewing the treats when someone mentioned licorice might help with the indigestion that was plaguing him as of late. It also seemed to help rid him of any aftertaste from long hours of pipe smoking and, as an added benefit, kept his breath fresh. Besides, he grown to enjoy the taste of the small candied bits.

Pedro Peralta was nowhere to be found inside the house, so Thad assumed he had simply gotten an early start on his morning chores. He took one last look around the cabin, reached up, and took down his Winchester from the pegs on the wall next to the door. Sighing, he opened the door and walked out toward the corral.

When he turned the corner, he found to his surprise that his was not the only horse saddled and ready to go. Pedro was sitting on his favorite *tobiano*, a large black-and-white pinto gelding. Thad noticed that his friend was wearing his old holster belt with a Remington Single Action .44 caliber revolver on one side and the old machete hanging down to the left. It had been years since Pedro had regularly worn that rig. McCallum immediately knew at a glance what it meant.

"Going somewhere, *muchacho*?" he asked suspiciously.

"*Sí, jefe*. I am going with you," Pedro answered firmly.

"Since when do I need a nursemaid, Pedro?" Thad asked his old friend.

"Yesterday I see an owl hopping on the ground and hooting during the day. Last night, too, there was a bird tapping on the window of your house. Then the sign over the main gate, she worked loose and fell down. Bad signs all. Pedro has a bad feeling about this trip. Better I should go with you."

"Oh, hell, you know I've been meaning to

re-nail that damned sign for months. It was just a matter of time before it fell off. And since when are you worried about a damned owl?" McCallum asked as if annoyed.

"The owl was outside, hooting during the day-time, that's why. And the sign, why she took all this time only to suddenly fall off now? No, these are bad omens." Pedro was insistent, stubborn.

After all these years McCallum knew better than to argue with his friend, especially when it came to his superstitions. Besides, deep down, Thad knew he would enjoy having some company on the trip.

"But what about the ranch?" he asked, feigning anger.

"We already had the spring roundup and I checked last night with Drago. He can handle things right good. The bank will give him credit for anything that comes up," Pedro assured Thad.

Drago Wilson was one of their oldest wranglers and a very dependable man. He was widely known as a man of true sand who would ride for the brand whenever necessary. It was hard to argue with Pedro about Drago's ability to handle the job.

"Damn, you are one obstinate old lady," Thad said, shaking his head. "All right, dammit, I guess you can mosey along with me." He slid his Winchester rifle into his saddle scabbard.

The old *vaquero* just looked back at him firmly and nodded. There had never been any doubt in Pedro's mind about whether he would go. If necessary, he had been prepared to wait until McCallum rode out, and then follow him at a distance.

McCallum didn't want to put anyone in jeopardy because of his personal obligations, let alone his old friend. Also, it bothered him that Pedro was acting as though he felt Thad couldn't handle things by himself any more. The last thing McCallum needed now was a worrywart mothering him. However, despite all this, deep inside, he was glad to have his old companion riding along.

McCallum took up his reins and started to mount. When he flexed his knees, he suddenly felt the early morning weakness typical of arthritis. He grunted and walked the horse over to a mounting block he had built a year or so ago. It was basically nothing more than a box fashioned into a couple of wooden steps, but it helped make it simpler for kids, women, and apparently, now, old men to mount up.

He looked around, embarrassed, climbed the steps, and swung his leg over the horse. He adjusted his round-brimmed campaign hat with the four-corner Montana crease and cleared his throat as if to redirect attention away from his deficiency.

"Well, if we're going, we might as well get on with it," he said sharply.

"*Vamanos*," replied the old *vaquero*, putting a soft spur to his horse.

It was a two-hour uneventful ride to the railhead. When they finally arrived at the station, McCallum noticed it was a little more crowded than usual. The two men rode to the ticket window of the El Paso and Southwestern Railroad Company. McCallum dismounted and handed his reins to his friend.

"Two tickets to Columbus," McCallum said, sliding a couple of bills through the window slot. "We'll be needing passage for our horses, also."

The ticket manager nodded and made change. He slid the change back to McCallum, then the two tickets. "The livestock cars are at the back of the train. Just show the conductor your tickets."

Thad took his reins back from Pedro and they walked their horses toward the end of the trai . They took their place in the back of a line of men waiting to board their horses and mules.

The two livestock cars had wooden ramps leading up into them where stalls had been built. Straw lined the floors and there were small wooden troughs for hay. Water buckets were securely hung inside each stall.

Things seemed to be proceeding as needed when suddenly a stranger, leading a chestnut horse, butted his way into the front of the line, shoving another passenger aside.

McCallum mentally recorded his appearance almost by reflex. The man, who was a stranger to him, was of average build, wore a fedora creased fore to aft, and was wearing a long brown jacket. He sported a large mustache and had a small scar under his left eye.

The intruder tried to lead his horse up the ramp much too quickly and, not surprisingly, the animal spooked. Instead of backing up and reassuring his horse, the man raised his voice and jerked even harder on the bridle.

Horses are herd animals and are used to the soft tactile responses of other members of their herd. Loud noises and pain represent a warning and create a fear response. This stranger obviously either didn't know this or didn't care, and when the horse began whinnying and continued backing up, the man pulled out a quirt from under his coat and began whipping the poor animal.

"Move it, you dumb beast, I'm in a hurry!" he shouted angrily.

McCallum watched him use the long crop a couple of times more, sighing in disgust to himself. He then turned and again handed his reins to his companion.

"Here, hold these, Pedro," he instructed. Looking up, he noticed a large branch that hung directly in front of the ramp. Reaching over, Thad pulled a lariat from his saddle and tied the long end around his saddle horn. He then tossed the rest of the rope over the tree limb and caught it by the looped end. Walking up quietly behind the poor animal's abuser, he tossed the rope over the man's neck and quickly tightened the noose.

Almost at the same time Pedro backed up the big black horse. This in turn created more tension on the rope. Since the lariat was directed down from the tree branch, essentially the pulley effect could hang the man. He went up on his toes and was forced to stay there. To struggle any more would mean a broken neck.

McCallum went over to the frightened horse and began rubbing his hand gently along the chestnut's neck. He slowly removed his coat and gently placed it over the animal's head, creating the same effect as a set of blinkers. The old cavalryman spoke soothingly as he led the horse up and into the car and tied him into a stall. Once back outside of the livestock car, he glanced at Pedro.

"O.K., that should be enough, I reckon."

Peralta loosened the rope from around the saddle horn and the man collapsed to the ground face first, coughing and gagging. McCallum removed the rope's noose from around the man's head, bent over, and murmured in his ear:

"If I ever hear of you beating a horse like that again, I'll come back and finish this little necktie party. Might even quirt you first. Now you just remember that."

The stranger was writhing on the ground, choking too much to reply, but Thad assumed he had gotten the drift of his warning.

Pedro walked up and McCallum replaced the lariat on his saddle. Then the two led their horses into the livestock car with little effort. Once they had assured themselves that the horses were well stabled, McCallum pulled his Winchester from its scabbard and the two men went forward to the nearest passenger car.

Chapter Four

When the train finally pulled out, McCallum and Peralta were seated in the back of their passenger car. Pedro was once again whittling on a small stick while Thad had the usual pipe in his mouth, billowing enough smoke to be in competition with the engine. Propped on the seat next to him was McCallum's ever-present Winchester rifle.

After they had been under way for a while, Thad set down his pipe and then lowered the window shade. Reclining back in his seat, he pulled down the brim of his campaign hat and took a nap. If he had learned anything in the cavalry, it was to grab as much sleep as you can when you can. One never knew when the next opportunity for sleep might occur while out in the field.

After a spell, McCallum woke up. Pedro was still whittling the stick that was now much thinner. He was also smoking a hand-rolled cigarette.

"Don't expect anything exciting happened while I was out?" McCallum asked.

Pedro shook his head. "*Nada*. The train stopped for water a short time ago. Only other thing was a small boy carrying a *charola* . . . a tray of candy, fruit, and tobacco. He went through to the next car."

Thad nodded. "Catch him when he comes back. I should fill up my tobacco pouch while I can." He arched himself and stretched out his arms to ease the stiffness in his lower back. Opening the shade, he glanced out. Almost immediately he noticed the shadows cast on the ground from the train top. Perhaps it was his years as a detective or his natural curiosity that got the better of him, but McCallum was troubled by what he had seen. He raised the window way up, took off his hat, and stuck his head out the opening.

Pedro was curious. "Whatcha doing, *jefe*? Getting a breath of fresh air?"

McCallum shook his head. "Thought I saw something funny. Hold on a second," he said. Looking back, and then forward again, Thad finally saw what was making the shadows on the ground as the train traveled along. Pulling his head in, he turned to his friend. "We've got company."

"How's that?" Pedro asked.

"There's at least two men up on the roof. If it was just one man, it might be a railroad employee, but two, right after a water tower stop? It has to mean a robbery is in progress."

"So, what do we do?" the *vaquero* asked. Unconsciously Pedro had begun fingering the grip on his pistol.

McCallum looked at him a moment before answering. "Oh, I suppose some damned old fool's gotta go up there after 'em."

"How many times have you told me that, when you were in the Army, they always told you never to volunteer for anything? Eh, *jefe*?" Pedro joked, removing his pistol and checking its cylinder.

McCallum stood and picked up his Winchester. He lengthened its sling and put the rifle over his shoulder. He shrugged. "Well, if we don't do this, who will?" He pointed to his hat lying on the seat bench. "Keep an eye on that. Don't much fancy having it blown off up there."

"Be careful up there, *jefe*. Your knees . . . they aren't what they used to be."

"Oh, go screw yourself," Thad replied angrily. "Yours aren't any better than mine." Even so, deep down he knew his friend was right. "Anyone comes through that door who isn't carrying a candy tray," Thad continued, "you'll probably need to shoot. Just be careful. I don't want to have to break in a new foreman."

Pedro nodded, got up, and went over to the bench seat that was nearest to the door at the front end of the compartment. He then sat down, put his pistol in his lap with his sombrero over it, and slid over toward the window, as far away from the door as possible. "*Suerte.* You be careful, *jefe*," he said.

"Good luck to you, too, *compadre*."

McCallum went out the back door of the railroad car and climbed the ladder to the roof. Before he brought his head fully into view, he peered cautiously over the top of the ladder. At the far end of the train he could see one man perched atop the first railroad car. But there was no sign of a second man.

Thad had no way of knowing how many robbers were on the train, but the man near the engine car had his handgun out and was aiming it at someone. Thad guessed he was pointing it at the engineer.

Since the robber was facing forward and occupied, McCallum unslung his rifle and went up on top. The effect of the moving train on his balance was stronger than he had expected and since the tracks curved from time to time the likelihood of a clean shot, even with a rifle, was slim to none.

He started walking the length of the car relatively upright, but almost immediately was blown sideways by the force of the wind. It was a miracle that he hadn't fallen. He was forced to squat down and duck-walk to keep his balance. Unfortunately, the strain that put on his knees was incredible and he cursed silently at the sharp pain. Forcing himself onward through sheer willpower, McCallum progressed over two more cars before lowering himself down the ladder located between the cars.

"The hell with this," he mumbled to himself.

At this distance, he felt he could finally make the shot, so, while steadying himself on the ladder, he lay the rifle down along the rail car's roof and adjusted the sling along his forearm.

When the train straightened after a curve, McCallum took a chance and fired. The robber stood up, arched as if in a spasm, and pitched sideways off the train. Thad knew at least one man was already inside the train, probably working his way through the cars if he hadn't yet realized what was happening above. And McCallum believed that his shot wouldn't have been heard, especially not with all the wind howling and the added noise of the locomotive. Even so he would take no chances. It was not in his nature to do so.

McCallum climbed down the ladder and started forward through the train compartments. At each door, he yelled: "Pinkerton Detective Agent, relax everyone!" He knew the rifle would startle most of the passengers and, although he technically wasn't an agent any more, the white lie might just save him from being shot by some frightened but armed rider.

Upon entering the third car forward in line, he came upon a robber collecting money and valuables from the passengers. He was easy to spot. For one thing, the bandanna he wore as a mask was a dead giveaway, as was the fact that he whirled with a pistol in his hand as soon as McCallum entered the car. Even turning as fast as he did, the robber was still no match for a Winchester rifle that was already cocked, loaded, and leveled forward.

The train robber lurched backward from the force of McCallum's rifle bullet and fell back, a hole in his chest, sprawling across an elderly lady, who promptly fainted.

Methodically McCallum cleared the rest of the forward cars, and then checked on the engineer who was scared but fortunately still in control of the train. Lowering the hammer on his Winchester, Thad then proceeded back toward the rear of the train.

When he was about three quarters of the way, a shot suddenly rang out and McCallum picked up his pace to the rear of the train. In truth, he was worried about his old companion.

Peralta was sitting in his seat with his old sombrero cradled on his lap when the rear door of the compartment crashed open. A robber wearing a blue bandanna tied around the lower half of his face entered, carrying a cocked pistol. He was also carrying a carpetbag in his left hand. Even with the mask Pedro immediately recognized him as the same man he and McCallum had roped earlier.

"Don't nobody move and you won't get hurt!"

the robber yelled. "Get out all your money and jewelry and put it in my bag. Anyone who don't put nothin' in it will get plugged. Hell, I'll plug ya if I even think you're holding out on me."

There were a few screams and gasps from the passengers, but most complied quietly. A loaded pistol is a mighty strong persuader and in most cases a public pacifier. The thief worked his way up the aisle till he was even with the bench Pedro was on.

"So, it's you. Where's your friend? I have a score to settle with . . ."

The robber wasn't given a chance to finish his sentence. Pedro simply raised his sombrero and shot the man, pointblank.

"You can settle up with him in hell, *señor.* I think sooner or later you see us both there." The man's body was lying face up on the floor.

A few moments later McCallum busted through the door at the front of the car, rifle barrel first, looking for his friend. He almost tripped over the robber's body, but he was relieved to see Pedro calmly replacing his hat. "What took you so long, *jefe*?" he asked calmly.

"Oh, I stopped to get some licorice from that kid with the candy tray," McCallum replied. "Everything went as planned in here, I see."

There was no smile on either man's face.

McCallum then pulled the alarm rope and the train came to a sudden stop. "Guess we should get the conductor and search everywhere before we proceed. Maybe return their possessions to the passengers? Care to come along?"

"*Sí, jefe. Vamanos*," Pedro replied, holstering his Remington pistol.

There had been four men involved in the attempted robbery; the fourth was found hiding in the stable car. The conductors tied him up after a brief lesson in railroad etiquette concerning robbers, and then cuffed his hands to a pair of big iron rings that were bolted into the wall as tie-downs for livestock. The battered robber wouldn't be comfortable for the rest of the ride, but he most certainly would be secure.

"Good to go?" asked the conductor.

McCallum nodded. "I think so, but it's your train."

The conductor leaned out of the car and waved a flag. The engineer, standing by the big train's engine, smiled and waved back at them before he climbed aboard. As the train picked up speed, cheers rang out from the passenger cars.

Chapter Five

Columbus, New Mexico was just a sleepy little border town, but most of its inhabitants felt that the place had good potential for growth. There was a detachment of approximately three hundred and fifty soldiers from the 13th Cavalry stationed at Camp Furlong on the outskirts of Columbus, which helped create a sense of security in the community, and although there was turmoil occurring in the country to the south of their border, it seemed of very little interest to all but the most politically minded of the local population.

In the center of town just off the main square there was a small but prosperous photography shop run by Jacob Shaw. This morning his nephew Jeff was out in front of the store busily helping his uncle load their equipment into the wagon for a trip just north of town. The previous week they had been asked to photograph a wedding today for the daughter of a prominent local cattle rancher.

Jeff had arrived a couple of months earlier to learn the trade. He was a bright and energetic lad, but relatively naïve about the ways of the world. However, Jeff was smart enough to recognize a potentially successful commercial opportunity. Ever since Matthew Brady had become famous for his photographs of the Civil War, there was an ever-growing demand for such services and for trained photographers.

Jeff was also a fan of writers such as Stephen Crane, and in the back of his mind he thought that he might someday like to be a combination of both reporter and photographer, a sort of photo-journalist. Jeff had very little, if any, knowledge of cameras and film, but his uncle had years of experience behind him and was fond of his nephew. When Jeff's father, Albert, wrote his brother about teaching the boy his trade, Jacob Shaw was both flattered and more than pleased to agree.

"Jeff, my boy," he said, "just leave that camera out there on the tripod for now while we finish packing the wagon. We'll put the camera in last. Last on, first off. Get it?"

"I get it, Uncle Jacob."

Photography was still relatively in its infancy. Cameras were bulky and the chemicals and film were just as crude. Good photographers, like Brady who had come up with the idea of a traveling dark room, had learned to use those deficiencies to create artistic shading and spectacular images. Jeff's uncle was not yet famous, but in Jeff's mind he clearly fell into the category of someone very worthy of learning from.

"You know, you should have written to your parents by now. It's not right to keep them in the dark," Jacob commented as he returned to the wagon.

Jeff lowered his head and shrugged. "I know, Uncle. I tried to send them a telegraph but it turned out all the lines were down. Then I was going to write them, but I kept telling myself the lines would be fixed soon, and since that would be quicker than sending a letter, I kept putting it off. Guess I was wrong. It's taken much longer than I thought it would."

"Ever heard the saying about never putting something off till tomorrow when you can do it today? You know, that's especially true when it comes to your family. Could've, should've, would've. No substitute for doing something right now, is there?"

Jeff shook his head slowly. "No, Uncle, I guess there isn't."

"O.K., then, as soon as we get back to town after this job, get that letter in the mail. Right now, though, it's time to get on with our business. So, while you finish with the wagon, I'm going to get my hat and coat and lock up the shop." Jacob patted Jeff's shoulder, and went inside.

Jeff confirmed that everything they needed was in the wagon, except for the large camera and its tripod. Emerging from the shop, Jacob Shaw put his hand above as eyes, as if he were saluting someone, and looked off into the distance. The expression on his face changed as if something bad had caught his attention.

"Something wrong, Uncle Jacob?" Jeff asked, curious.

"Look over there, boy. See the smoke? It looks as if there's some sort of fire over where that Army detachment is located."

"Huh. Wonder what's up? You suppose they could be burning trash?" Jeff asked.

His uncle shook his head. "This early in the morning? Not likely."

Just then a loose horse raced down the street, passing the two and heading out of town. Its neck was lathered up and the horse had a wild, frightened look in its eyes.

"Now what's that all about?" Jacob pondered aloud. "I wonder if the Army barn caught . . . ?"

A shot rang out and Jacob grabbed his right shoulder with his left hand, spun around, and fell to the ground.

"Uncle Jacob!" his nephew cried out. He barely had time to rush to the man's side before a group of Mexicans charged down the street, shooting their pistols into nearby store-fronts and windows.

Five of them brought their horses to a halt in front of Jeff, pointing their weapons right at him. Jeff, who like his uncle always went unarmed, backed up, stopping next to the tripod. He was sure the time had finally come for him to meet his Maker.

The lad often used his sarcastic sense of humor to get himself out of trouble, but he knew in this situation sarcasm would be of little use. Luckily, he had inherited some of his father's raw courage. And therefore, being Albert Shaw's only son, there was no way a bunch of Mexican hooligans would make him beg for his life. No way. Not after one of them had shot his uncle.

As he shifted, his hand brushed up against the camera's tripod. Jeff studied the group, slowly realizing they looked more like outlaws, not hooligans. Mexican *bandidos*. As he stood there, not knowing what to do, he remembered the advice of his father: *If and when you have no other choice, you might as well be brave.* Taking a deep breath, Jeff addressed the men in what he hoped was a calm but strong voice.

"So, which one of you wants his picture taken?" he asked, swallowing hard after he got the words out. He tried to smile, but deep down he was feeling very unsure of the situation. He pointed at the camera, lifted its curtain, directing the men's attention to the cord that triggered the camera. "*¿Tomo tus fotos, muchachos?*" He repeated his previous question, but this time in Spanish as he tried to remember the basics of the language he had learned as a boy from his Cuban nursemaid.

Although Jeff could barely keep his knees from buckling as the outlaws stared back at him, he was determined to go out standing straight, looking death in the eye. He wasn't sure if he could pull it off, but he felt confident that this was what his father would do in such a situation, and it was what he would expect his son to do as well.

A cloud of dust suddenly swirled as another Mexican galloped up the street. He pulled hard on his reins, putting his horse into a sliding stop in front of the men. This man wore a large black-and-white sombrero and across his chest he was wearing bandoleers full of ammunition. He had a rather round face and wore his mustache long over his lightly whiskered face. Although he appeared of average build, his presence was commanding, as indicated by the five men who, upon his arrival, turned toward him as if awaiting his instructions.

So far Jeff hadn't been shot, so he decided to continue with his ploy.

"¿Foto, señor?" he repeated.

The man, who perhaps was the leader, stared at Jeff, studying him. He then burst out laughing. "At least this *muchacho* has a pair of balls on him," he said in Spanish to the other men. They all broke out laughing, and Jeff, even though he hadn't understood exactly what had been said, relaxed a mite and smiled nervously. After all, he was grateful to still be alive since he could hear shooting in other parts of town.

"You know, it might not be a bad idea to have someone taking some pictures of all our victories," the leader said in Spanish. The man seemed to mull over the idea. "Grab this *gringo*, get his wagon and the crap that's in it, and bring him along," he ordered. "¡*Vamanos*!"

"*Sí, mi general*," the men replied almost in unison.

The use of the term "general" got Jeff's attention. What would bandits be doing with a general? he wondered.

Two of the men jumped from their horses, grabbed him, and practically tossed him up onto the buckboard's seat. They then picked up the camera.

"Hey, careful with that . . . um . . . *cuidado*!" Jeff yelled.

The two looked at him angrily, but obeyed him, gently placing the camera into the wagon. Then they tied his hands and feet.

Jeff could hear shots being fired throughout the city, and, as he looked around, he saw smoke billowing from a fire springing up just a few blocks away.

One of the *bandidos* climbed up onto the wagon seat and used a whip to start the buckboard's team. Soon more men began joining them as they headed south out of town.

After they had passed Columbus' town limits, Jeff estimated he was riding with an army of about a hundred men. They were armed to the teeth, and some were leading a herd of horses and mules, most likely stolen from the fort Jeff surmised. There were also several wagons loaded down with boxes. Since the crates all had Army markings on them Jeff assumed they were filled with ammunition and weapons of some sort.

As the group approached the border with Mexico, a loud cheer rang out: "¡*Viva Méjico*! ¡*Viva Villa*!"

Chapter Six

After their train pulled into the station located just outside of town, McCallum and Peralta were approached by the head conductor.

"I'm sure the railroad will want to offer you men some sort of reward. Want to leave your names and addresses with me?" the man asked.

There might have been a time when McCallum would have taken pride in his accomplishment, but not now. All Thaddeus McCallum wanted from life was peace and quiet. These days he didn't like to be disturbed. Besides, the robbers might have friends and he didn't want to bring any of them into his life.

Thad knew his friend well enough to know Pedro would feel the same. He looked at the conductor and shook his head. "Nope. If there's any reward, just divide it evenly among the crew. They deserve something for the risks they take and for helping out this time."

"You sure?" the conductor asked, surprised.

McCallum and Pedro both nodded.

"Well, then, thanks a lot," the railroad man said sincerely. He offered his hand in gratitude. "And you both have a safe journey now, hear?"

"Try to. Besides, after this what more can go wrong?" McCallum joked.

After a short ride the two men finally approached the town of Columbus. Thad knew that there was an Army detachment in the area, the 13th he believed, but he was still surprised to find a sentry posted this far outside of town. McCallum was a little annoyed when they were braced by him.

"Halt! Who goes there?" the sentry asked with a crack in his voice. He looked to be no more than seventeen and in McCallum's judgment still wet behind the ears.

Pedro raised his hand to his face to cover a smile. Thad took a different tack.

"Soldier," he snapped, "when you address someone while on sentry duty, say it like you god-damned well mean it. You sound like a frightened kid at the schoolmarm's blackboard. Clear your damned throat before you speak."

The soldier just looked at him in astonishment.

"And why ask the damned question in the first place if you don't have the wherewithal to back it up? Take the damned safety off your rifle."

"Er . . . yes, sir," the lad replied, fumbling with his rifle.

"And don't sir me, soldier. I work for a living."

"Yes, sir," he replied before he could correct himself.

McCallum just stared at him and shook his head in frustration.

"Look, sonny, I used to wear that same uniform but for a hell of a lot longer than you have. So why don't you just explain to me what the Sam Hill a sentry is doing on duty way out here in front of a peaceful little American town?"

This time the soldier cleared his throat first before answering. Pedro had to stifle a laugh. Over the years riding with McCallum he had seen variations of this routine repeated many times.

"Well, far as they tell me, this here's now a war zone. See we was attacked a couple of days ago," the sentry explained.

"Attacked?" Thad repeated. "Out here? By who? A couple of little old ladies on their way to church in a buckboard?"

"Oh, no, sir. By Mexicans! A whole army," the soldier answered, looking somewhat sheepishly at the *vaquero*.

Peralta was expressionless. "*Revolucionarios*," he whispered. "Must be, *jefe*."

McCallum shrugged. "Anything else gonna go wrong on this damned trip?" He looked up, inhaled, noticing for the first time the smell of the smoke lingering in the air. "How badly did they burn the place up?"

"Well, sir, it's like this," the soldier said, lowering his rifle. "They burned quite a bit. Word is they killed almost twenty men. Stole a lot of horses and guns, too. Leastwise that's what they tell me."

"Private, just where is your sergeant stationed now? And stop calling me sir. I ain't no damned officer."

The young soldier nodded. "Once you get into town, turn right, and go all the way down to the camp. It's located about ten blocks west."

McCallum nodded. "Thanks, Private." As they started to leave, McCallum paused a moment. "On second thought, maybe you should leave the rifle's safety on, after all. Wouldn't want you to shoot yourself." With that the two men rode on to the town.

As they rode in to Columbus, they studied the people milling around in the street. As far as Thad was concerned there was far too much activity and noise for a town this size. It was as if everyone and everything had been set in motion at the same time.

"Looks bad, *jefe*," Pedro commented.

Thad didn't reply. He just scanned the streets as if looking for something he might use to his own benefit. It was an old habit. His eyes finally came to rest on an Army detail of five soldiers who were carrying water pails. He and Pedro rode over to them.

"We're looking for the sergeant. Know where we can find him?" McCallum asked. In his experience sergeants usually ran the Army at the local level, used to dealing with the down and dirty on a daily basis. Ask specifically for the sergeant, and odds are you'd get the real person in charge.

The oldest of the men set down his pails and looked up at the two men on horseback. He recognized the kind of hat McCallum was wearing as old Army issue and was a little curious as to why the man would be riding with a Mexican. He took out a handkerchief and wiped his brow.

"Top kick's over at the supply depot," he explained. "Go down this street and turn left when you go past the ladies' dress shop. It'll be down at the far end."

"Thanks, soldier," McCallum replied, tossing him a relaxed salute.

The depot was indeed a beehive of activity. Soldiers were coming and going in a way that to the untrained eye might seem rather chaotic. As McCallum saw it, however, there clearly was a method in all this madness.

"Mobilizing," he said to Pedro.

"For what, *jefe*?"

"From the way it looks to me, the Army's gonna get involved in whatever this is . . . big time. Wouldn't surprise me if they didn't work this up to a full-scale expedition."

"The whole Army for such a little attack?" Pedro asked.

McCallum thought for a moment, then nodded his head. "Looks like it to me."

The two men dismounted and tied their horses to a nearby hitching post. They then walked into the depot and looked around. It was a big barn-like affair with two large sliding doors both at the front and rear of the building. Off to the left side were two long wooden tables and several chairs. There was an American flag nailed to the wall behind them. A soldier with several stripes on his arms was seated at the first table, handing out papers to a line of men gathered in front of him.

"Follow me," Thad said to his friend.

As the two approached the tables, they watched a young man step up and address the sergeant. He was in civilian clothing.

"Excuse me, sir?" the boy said. "I'd like to speak with someone about enlisting. Would it be you I talk to?" he asked.

"As good as anyone I suppose," the sergeant replied, looking up from his stack of papers. "What do you want to know?"

"Well, my family had some friends killed in the attack and I want to do my part. Problem is, I'm not sure about going into the Army. My uncle says the Marines is better," the lad commented sheepishly.

"That so?" the sergeant said, looking the boy over, top to bottom.

By now McCallum and Peralta had moved up to wait their turn. They couldn't help overhearing the conversation.

"Yes, sir," said the young man. "See, I just cain't make up my mind. You Army fellows is closer, but some says the Navy gets better chow, and others told me where the Marines are . . . well, that's where the action is."

McCallum couldn't help a smile taking shape on his face, knowing the boy was setting himself up for a good leg pulling from the sergeant.

The sergeant studied the boy a bit before saying: "Well, let me ask you a question, young man. Are your parents married . . . and were they married to each other when you was born?"

The lad looked puzzled by the question and was obviously bothered by the sergeant's insinuation.

"Yes, sir!" he replied angrily. "Of course they were. Married right and proper, too."

The sergeant smiled, arching his eyebrow.

At this point, McCallum nudged his friend to get his attention. "Listen to this one, Pedro," he whispered.

"Well, then it isn't even an issue for ya," the sergeant explained.

"How so?" the lad asked, turning red under the soldier's gaze.

"I'll explain it to you, son. See, iffen your parents was married to each other when you was born, why then you just simply won't qualify for the Navy or the Marines."

McCallum had to choke back a laugh. He had

said just about the same thing himself to nervous recruits on several occasions.

The sergeant handed the lad a piece of paper and pointed to another table across the room. "Fill this out, and then take it to the soldier at that table over there and he'll get things started for you. Welcome to the Army, boy. We'll make a man out of you yet."

The young man stared at the paper in his hand with a blank expression. After some hesitation, he turned and headed to the other side of the depot.

Moving up in line, McCallum unbuttoned his coat and took off his gloves. "Sorry to bother you, Sarge," he said bluntly, "but might I ask what the hell's going on here?"

The sergeant looked up at McCallum, glaring at him for his impertinence. At first sight the man might have been mistaken for someone a bit too overweight, but McCallum knew at a glance that stocky would have been a much better description. McCallum had witnessed the strength of many such barrel-chested men over the years. This one was probably capable of bending horseshoes with his bare hands if he desired.

"Who wants to know?" the sergeant said suspiciously. "I ain't got a lot of time to waste."

"Name's McCallum. Ex-sergeant Thaddeus McCallum."

The sergeant did a double take. "No shit? I heard of you. You the one they used to call the Iron Sergeant way back when?"

"Well, far as I'm concerned, with all the cuts and bruises I got over the years, nothing qualifies me for anything even remotely made of iron."

"Not the way I heard it. You're the same McCallum who charged up the Hill with Roosevelt, ain't you?" the sergeant asked.

"Geez, you had to have been just a kid back then," McCallum said, shaking his head in amazement. "Surprised anyone still remembers."

"I was old enough for my first hitch," the man replied proudly.

"Yeah, I made the climb all right," McCallum explained. "I was actually on Leonard Wood's staff, but I got attached temporarily to Colonel Teddy's group for the assault. Not really much charging, though. Mostly just falling and crawling. In all the confusion, I ended up right next to Lieutenant Black Jack Pershing."

"Blackjack?" Pedro asked, curious.

"John J. Pershing," Thad explained. "He was the lieutenant in charge of the Tenth Cavalry, a Negro outfit. The buffalo soldiers. Jack is a nickname for John. It was a black unit he commanded, thus Black Jack Pershing."

"Don't let the old man hear you call him that now," the sergeant replied, grinning. "The general's in charge of this whole shebang. This here's gonna be a real damned expedition. President Wilson ordered it himself."

"From snot-nosed lieutenant all the way up to general. Who'd've thought it? Man's got guts, though, I'll give him that," McCallum remarked more to Pedro than to the sergeant.

"He better have, iffen he's gonna lead all this," the sergeant observed, nodding his head in agreement. "My name's Lucas. Travis . . . no middle name . . . Lucas," he added.

"How bad we get hit, Sarge?" McCallum asked.

"As far as I can tell, we lost eighteen, maybe nineteen and had another some odd wounded. They got away with about a hundred of our stock. Damned beaners attacked us at early light. Hit us first, and then went for the town. Charged right in and shot up the place."

Pedro was obviously bothered by the "beaner" slur, but Thad put a hand on his friend's arm as a caution. "Not the time or place," he warned in a whisper. Then, turning back to the soldier, he said: "Look, Sarge, I'm not trying to take up much of your time here. We're just looking for a friend. Young lad who was working as a photographer in town. Jeff Shaw's the name. Any idea where I might find him?"

The sergeant reached for a piece of paper on the far side of his table and started running his finger down the names it listed. It was obviously the casualty list. When he paused for a moment,

Thad had a sinking feeling, but the sergeant looked up and shook his head. "Sorry, no Shaw on this list."

"Any idea where the photography shop in town might be?"

"No, but check with the corporal over there. The damned fool spends more time walking around town than he does working."

"Thanks."

"Glad to be of help," the sergeant said, nodding. "Now let me get back to straightening out all the brass's problems like I always do."

McCallum laughed. "Nothing ever changes, does it? Well, keep your head down, your pecker covered, and your powder dry." He then crossed the room and addressed the corporal who was rolling a cigarette.

The difference between the sergeant and this younger man was immediately obvious. Old school versus new school. The corporal was a rather lanky sort, about twenty-five years of age. His tie had been loosened and the top button on his shirt was undone. By contrast, even in all the dust and heat, the sergeant's uniform had looked like it just came from a Chinese laundry. The corporal on the other hand looked like he didn't even know what a laundry was.

"Got a minute, Corporal?"

"Sure, what's up?" he replied suspiciously.

"The sergeant felt you might be the one who

could direct us to the town's photography shop."

The corporal seemed relieved. "That all? Sure, no problem. Follow me." They walked to the depot's front opening. Pointing, the corporal said: "Just go back up the street here and, when you get to the dress shop, keep going straight for three blocks and then turn right. It's on the left-hand side."

"Got it," McCallum replied.

"Want I should take you there?" the corporal asked.

McCallum glanced over at the old *vaquero* with a smirk. "No thanks. We can take it from here. Besides, the sergeant mentioned something about needing your help." The sergeant hadn't said anything of the kind.

"He did?" the corporal asked. He sounded nervous.

"*Sí, señor*," Pedro replied, nodding.

"I'd straighten that tie and button your tunic first, if I were you," McCallum added. "The sergeant sounded annoyed."

"Right, thanks. I'm on it."

"Sure, you are," Thad replied sarcastically.

For all his lack of work ethic, at least the corporal's directions proved reliable. Pedro was the first to spot the photo shop and the man standing out in front.

"See his shoulder, *jefe*?" Pedro remarked.

The man he'd pointed out was wearing a sling

around his right shoulder and arm. His head was lowered and he seemed lost in thought.

"Excuse me," Thad said, walking up to the shop. "I am looking for the photographers who work here. In particular, I'm trying to find Jeffery Shaw."

The man sighed deeply. "That's my nephew. I'm his uncle, Jacob Shaw."

Thad started to reach out to shake hands, but he observed that the man winced in pain as he shifted to shake with his left hand. He stopped himself and simply nodded instead.

"Pleased to meet you. I'm Thad McCallum and this is my friend, Pedro Peralta."

The man looked at Thad and studied him for a moment. "I've heard of you," he said. "You were in the Army with my brother Al, right?"

"Yes, sir, I was. Good man."

Shaw smiled. "That he is. How can I help you? What's this about Jeff? Why are you looking for him?"

McCallum explained: "Your brother asked us to find Jeff because he was concerned for his welfare. Apparently, Al tried but couldn't get in touch with him. Seems he hasn't heard from him for a while."

Jacob Shaw nodded. "I fussed at Jeff about that, too. Then the telegraph lines went out. The lad was fine till all this happened." Shaw looked up the street and shrugged.

"Was?" McCallum asked.

"Well, when the Mexicans attacked, we were both out in front of the shop. Jeff was working on loading the wagon when I was shot." Jacob touched his right shoulder. "I hit the ground and that's the last thing I remember. I came to in the doc's office where he had patched me up, but Jeff never came looking for me. I had hoped he was guarding the store, but when I got here, there was no sign of him. Nothing. And the equipment, supplies, including my best camera, are all gone, along with the buckboard. I figured the horses spooked and ran off, what with all the shooting those Mexicans were doing."

"Well, Jeff's not on the casualty list," Thad commented.

Shaw nodded. "I know. I already checked."

"So, where is he?" Pedro asked.

"I simply don't know and I must admit I'm very worried," Shaw replied.

"There must be something you remember. Any little thing might help," Thad said.

"Well, like I said . . . I don't remember much."

The detective in McCallum began to kick in. "No sign of Jeff, and your wagon and the equipment in it are gone. Maybe the bandits took your stuff. But ask yourself, what's the likelihood that someone in a bunch of bandits knows how to use a camera and a bunch of other photography equipment?"

"Not much," Shaw responded.

"*Revolucionarios*," Pedro suggested at this point.

"What?" the two other men asked in unison.

"These are not *bandidos, jefe*," Pedro responded. "Too well organized, too many men." He shook his head. "During the attack, they were focused on getting guns, ammunition, and horses at the fort. I think here, in Columbus, they were just trying to scare the people by shooting up the town and killing those who got in their way. They didn't even try to rob the banks."

McCallum thought a moment, staring off in the distance. "Planned just like a military raid. Take out the opposing army by surprise, and then put the fear of God in the civilians."

"*Sí*, and they left the women alone," Pedro pointed out. "*Bandidos*, they don't act like that."

"*Revolucionarios*," the two men concluded together.

Chapter Seven

Jacob Shaw invited the two men into his shop. "Would either of you care for a cup of coffee?" he asked.

Both men nodded. "Hot, black, and strong," McCallum said.

"Take me a moment. Flying with one wing so to speak," Shaw said, before disappearing into a room in the back.

When he returned, Shaw held a pot in his left hand. He went over to a small stove located in the corner of his shop and set the pot down. He fumbled with the stove's door, then tried to get a match out of his pocket.

"Here, let me help you with that," Pedro offered, striking a match and tossing it into the stove.

"So, what do you reckon happened to my nephew?" Shaw asked.

McCallum hesitated a moment as if considering the possibilities.

"Army's pretty good about taking body counts, so if we assume they are correct and he wasn't among the dead, then the logical answer is that he was taken out of town."

"But why?" Shaw asked. "He's got nothing to offer them, no money to speak of. Nothing."

"The camera stuff, she's missing, too," Pedro reminded.

McCallum nodded. "Right. So why would they want a photographer?" he asked, pouring coffee into three tin cups.

"A photographer? Jeff hardly learned anything," Shaw informed them. "He'd only been with me a short time."

"But they wouldn't know that, now, would they?" McCallum asked.

Shaw and Pedro both shook their heads.

"So, what would an army of revolutionaries need with a photographer?"

"If it was Villa, he likes the attention," Pedro explained. "He is the sort who wants the whole world to see him."

"Villa?" Thad asked, sipping his coffee.

"*Sí*. Pancho. His real name is José Doroteo Arango Arámbula," Peralta explained. "They call him Francisco like his *abuelo*, his grandfather. Pancho is short . . . you know, a nickname . . . for Francisco."

"So, who the hell is he?" McCallum asked.

"He was the *caudillo* of the state of Chihuahua. A very powerful man," Peralta said.

"*¿Caudillo?*" Shaw asked, puzzled.

"*Sí*. It means leader. Like a governor would be here."

"And you think this Villa fellow was behind all this?" McCallum asked.

Peralta nodded his agreement. "He was very involved in the revolution but now he does not like President Carranza and so he formed his own army, *La Division del Norte*. Some say he has between five hundred and a thousand men following him. *Villaistas* they are called. Now they fight to overthrow Carranza."

"So why would he want to attack our town? Why attack Americans? We ain't done nothing to him," Shaw asked angrily.

Peralta thought a moment. "Our President, *Señor* Wilson, he used to support Villa, but then he stopped sending guns and switched over to *Presidente* Carranza's side. Maybe Pancho is angry? You know, maybe he felt betrayed by the *gringos* and wants the *venganza* . . . revenge. Or maybe it is simply that he needs guns and bullets for his men? Maybe."

"Good a reason as any," McCallum commented.

"And Jeff?" Shaw asked.

"Maybe Villa wants pictures of his exploits?" Pedro replied.

"Your nephew," McCallum asked. "He the clever type?"

"What do you mean?" Shaw asked.

"Well, I was just thinking. If it came down to life or death, he might have pretended to be more than he really is. You know, to buy himself some more time. What do you think?"

"Makes sense, *jefe*," Pedro remarked, nodding.

"Let me get this straight," Shaw said. "You think Jeff was taken along with this Villa fellow to document his army's fight for the revolution with photographic pictures?"

Pedro nodded and Thad shrugged.

"Brady practically documented the Civil War," McCallum pointed out. "No reason not to believe that Villa might want Jeff to do the same thing."

"But he hardly knows how to work the camera," Jacob countered.

"Well, if he wants to stay alive, he better be a quick learner," Thad replied grimly.

"Looks like somebody's gonna be riding south, eh, *jefe*?" said Pedro.

McCallum sighed deeply, his stomach was beginning to ache. He reached for a licorice in his pocket. His dyspepsia was acting up again, as it often did when he was stressed.

"And we know who that somebody is gonna be, don't we, Pedro?" he said, looking at his friend.

"Good thing one of us knows how to *hablar Español*," Pedro pointed out.

McCallum turned to Jacob Shaw and put a hand on his shoulder.

"Pedro's right. It looks like we're going to be headed south into Mexico. If there is a chance in hell of getting the boy back, we'll do our best. I owe Al and Maggie that much."

"I don't know what to say," Jacob replied. "Wish I could go with you, but with this shoulder I'd be more hindrance than help," he said, rubbing his wound again.

"No problem. Never even thought to ask," Thad replied. "By the way, you need to move that arm even if it hurts. Not enough to open the wound, mind you, but if you let it set too long, the muscles will tighten up and whither on you. Got to keep 'em exercised. Might hurt at first, but you'll regret it later, iffen you don't."

"Thanks. I'll remember that," Shaw said.

Thad looked around the shop. "Would you happen to have a picture of the lad we could have? Might come in handy identifying him when we catch up with them."

Shaw nodded. "Matter of fact I took a few of him just last week." He walked over to his desk and rummaged around in one of its drawers before finding the photograph he was looking for. "Here, take this one. Hope it helps."

McCallum took the picture and put it in his shirt pocket. He and Pedro put down their coffee cups and reassured Shaw they would do everything they could to find his nephew. Then they left the shop.

"What now, *jefe*?" Pedro asked once they were outside.

"Well, it looks like the soldiers aren't the only ones who're gonna prepare an expedition," Thad said, thinking out loud. "But we've got to move fast. We'll need supplies, a couple of good pack mules, and maps."

"Where we gonna find maps of Mexico here?" Pedro asked.

Thad thought that over. "Our friends in the Army will surely be thinking the same thing. They're bound to have what we need. The trick is going to be to get them to give us one."

"Why don't we just ride with them? You know, go along with the Army expedition?"

McCallum shook his head. "If I learned one thing in uniform, it's that nothing in the Army gets done today. With Pershing in charge, they are bound to do this up big. And that means complicated. They'll take a lot of time to plan and prepare before they finally mobilize and move out."

"And that's gonna take too long?" Peralta wondered.

"I ask you, which moves faster, a single horse or a herd of buffalo? I'll bet you dollars to doughnuts this expedition is gonna make a herd of buffalo look tiny by comparison."

"There is safety in numbers, they say," Peralta pointed out.

"If this was your son, would you want me to wait?" Thad asked his friend.

Pedro shrugged and shook his head. "No, *jefe*, I guess not."

McCallum sucked on another licorice. "Well, there's no time like the present, so where do we start?" he asked.

"Horses and mules come first. Then we buy supplies, eh?" Pedro said.

"O.K., let's go find a stable," Thad replied.

Chapter Eight

It had been a couple of days of hard riding, usually with the dust from a hundred riders blowing back over Jeff Shaw's buckboard. Each night Jeff was separated from his wagon and guarded by two men with rifles.

As much as he thought about it, he could find no way of escaping. He certainly couldn't get away on a wagon. There simply wasn't one with enough speed for him to escape successfully. And even if he could somehow evade his guards and steal a fast horse, Jeff had no idea where he was or how to get back across the border.

Not only that, Jeff knew his chances of finding food and water along the way were slim to none. Even if he did stumble into some small town, he didn't think it was likely they would help him. In fact, he thought they would turn him right back over to these men, whoever they were. Then things would only get a lot worse.

So far Jeff had been treated all right. He hadn't been abused so far and had been offered food and water. Obviously, the leader, the one they called *El General*, liked the idea of having a photographer along. It made sense that to stay alive Jeff would have to keep the general happy. Unfortunately, that meant taking good pictures—

and not just taking them, but developing them as well.

Jeff had all the photographic supplies he needed, but not the experience. Up till now he had helped his uncle develop only a very few pictures. Jeff prayed he could remember all the steps and in the right sequence. He spent almost all his time going over everything he had observed his uncle do back in the shop.

When he awoke the third morning, instead of being led back to his buckboard as had been the routine, Jeff was taken to a clearing where there was a group of the bandits milling around. The general was standing in their midst. He turned and addressed his prisoner.

"All right, *gringo*, time to earn your keep. Take our picture," he ordered in Spanish.

It was obvious to Jeff that he was being addressed, and he had caught the gist of what was being requested of him. He had to think fast.

"I'm sorry but I don't understand you," he said in English. *When in doubt, play dumb,* he thought. Jeff shrugged and shook his head.

Exasperated the general threw up his hands. "*Gringos estupidos.*" He turned to one of the men standing next to him. "Go get me someone who speaks his barbaric language."

One of the other men gestured at Jeff, pointing his hand like the muzzle of a gun. It was a universal sign anyone could understand. "Why don't we just shoot the son-of-a-bitch, General?" the man said in Spanish.

"No, Julio," the general answered. "Not yet. Just wait till they find me someone who speaks his damned language."

After a few minutes a woman pushed through the crowd. Jeff couldn't help himself. He just couldn't take his eyes off her. He noticed that most of the other men were staring at her, too.

The young woman was about five foot six and had long dark hair and eyes that burned a hole in Jeff's heart. He figured her to be roughly about his age, or perhaps a year or two younger. She was wearing a long brown skirt with high leather riding boots and a white blouse. Like many of the men she wore crossed ammunition belts over her chest and a single holster around her waist. She looked as though she knew how to use the pistol it held, but as far as Jeff was concerned, the wide belt just accentuated her thin waist and made her all the more attractive.

"Mercedes, you speak English. Tell this one I want our picture taken," the leader ordered.

"*Sí, mi General Villa*," Mercedes replied. The girl turned and looked at the prisoner. "You have a name?" she asked in English. As much as she resented *Americanos*, she couldn't help but notice he was a good-looking man.

Jeff smiled at her. "Sure do. It's Jeff."

"Jeff," she asked, pronouncing it more like "Yeff".

"Short for Jeffery," he said. "Jeffery Shaw, er . . . *señora*," he said, using the Spanish word for madam.

"It's *señorita*, not *señora*," she replied, flipping her hair back over her shoulder.

Jeff smiled broadly. "Even better. So, you're not married. Fine with me . . . *señorita*."

Mercedes Valdez de Guerrera was accustomed to such flirtations from other men, but her boyfriend, the one the general called Julio, wasn't pleased with it. Not at all.

Julio Cardenas was one of Pancho Villa's most trusted captains and was closely protective of his girlfriend. He didn't speak English but he could read body language, especially when it was so blatantly obvious.

"Let me shoot him now," Cardenas said to Villa.

Villa just smiled and shook his head. He raised his hand up. "Maybe later."

Mercedes couldn't help but feel a little flustered at Jeff's display of relief when he learned she wasn't married. Still, he was a *gringo* and she had work to do.

"General Villa wants you should take their picture now," she said.

Jeff had already thought this out. "His name's Villa, eh? Well, I can't. Not right now," he replied.

94

Mercedes looked at him with surprise. "What? You refuse to do so?"

"Oh, no," he said. "Please tell the general I want to. It's just that I need to check the equipment. I didn't pack the wagon. Your men did. And after so many days in the buckboard with all that dust and bouncing, I need to make sure everything works and nothing has been damaged. That will take a while. Once that's done, I can set up the camera, take the picture, and then finally develop the film."

The Mexicans seemed annoyed as Mercedes translated.

"Please tell General Villa that I want to do it right," Jeff pleaded. "To get good pictures, you know." He tried once again to think like his father, a man with far more experience with such things. "I'm sure after his great attack back there, he will want to cover more ground in case there are Americans following him. Maybe once we get more settled, I can do as he asks. Till then I want to care for my things, so I take photos worthy of such a great man. Tell him that, *señorita*, please."

Again, the *señorita* translated. Villa seemed to accept what she told him. He nodded.

"Mercedes," the general finally ordered, "let him check his supplies and camera when we next stop. In the meantime, I want you to stay with him in the wagon and teach the fool to speak like a *Cristiano*. Tell him I want him to take pictures of our campaign and I want that to happen soon." Next to him Julio Cardenas grunted in anger. He was clearly upset by Villa's decision.

When Mercedes explained Villa's orders to him, Jeff smiled broadly.

"Might take a while to learn Spanish, *señorita*. You'll have to spend a whole lot of time with me. I'm afraid I'm a pretty slow learner," he said happily.

She shook her head. "For your sake, you better learn quickly. Pancho Villa is not a man of . . . how you say? . . . patience. And my boyfriend is not, either."

"And just who is the lucky man?" Jeff asked.

Mercedes pointed at Captain Cardenas. "He's the one making the sign at you of the throat cutting."

Jeff stopped smiling. "Great. Thanks for the warning."

Over the next several days Jeff went through the wagon, making a big show of carefully checking the camera and all the equipment and supplies. As he examined each piece, he went over and over in his mind every step his uncle had taken while developing the photos. He also spent a lot of time listening to Mercedes as she tried to teach him Spanish.

Truthfully, he was mesmerized by her face and felt faint whenever she slowly rolled her lips while asking him to repeat words after her. *She has great lips,* he would think to himself every time he looked at her.

Jeff learned he was not traveling with a band of outlaws but rather with an army of revolutionaries who called themselves *La Division del Norte* or the Northern Division. Pancho Villa was their leader.

Wish the general needed a surveyor instead of a photographer, Jeff thought to himself one morning as he puttered with the equipment. *Nobody ever knows how or what the hell they're really doing. One man looks through a mounted telescope and a second holds a tall stick. I could fake that all day and night. Now, instead, they're going to expect camera flashes and real damned photographs.*

"I wouldn't need much to make a picture of you come out well," Jeff said to Mercedes that day when she appeared at the wagon. She seemed to soften a little and, despite herself, was flattered. Unconsciously she played with her hair, twirling it around her finger, but her answer was still as blunt as ever.

"You are not here to take pictures of me. You must take a good one of Villa and his army, and soon or they will line you up and shoot you," she warned.

"Right," Jeff replied glumly.

Chapter Nine

After getting directions to the Columbus livery stable, Thad and Pedro found its caretaker out front. Thad asked him if there were any mules for sale.

The man was leaning on a pitchfork, near the barn's door. He was a short, bandy-legged type with a scruffy triangular chin beard.

"Well, sir, it's like this. What you ask is gonna be kinda hard now that the Army's in a buying mood."

McCallum thought about that for a moment and, taking an educated guess, replied: "Of course, any good stockman always holds back some when the market gets like this." He looked over the man's shoulder into the barn. "That way he can pawn off the rough, unbroken ones, the weak, and the cold bloods when the buyers are hot. Then, later, he will sell the stronger ones and the purebreds for a higher price when good stock is even more scarce."

"That so?" the liveryman said, spitting a stream of tobacco juice onto the ground. "What of it?"

"Well, if that were the case, and there was good stock held back, we'd be interested in buying two pack mules," McCallum said.

The man just stared at him without saying anything.

McCallum knew that look. He'd been a horse trader for too long not to. He reached into his pants pocket and pulled out a wallet from which he retrieved several bills. "If that were the case, that is. And then only for good solid stock."

The man's eyes dilated when he saw the money and he cracked a small smile. "Might be there still are some around, like you say."

"So, are we gonna pussyfoot around all day, or are you gonna make a quick profit?" McCallum asked.

"Well, you know . . . like I said . . . the Army's paying pretty good," the stableman remarked, still eyeing the cash.

McCallum nodded. "All we need is two mules and we will pay you well. But before you get too greedy, know this. My friend here has raised and trained horses and mules all his life. You try to put anything over on us and my next stop is going to be the veterinary's office."

"What for?" he asked.

"Well, I expect it won't take too much of this," he said, thumbing the bills in his hand, "to bribe him into quarantining this place for something like . . . say hoof and mouth disease." It was a total shot in the dark. McCallum didn't even know if the town had a permanent veterinarian.

The liveryman looked uncomfortable. "He wouldn't do that."

"It'd be a lot of money for a poor old horse doctor. You so sure?" Pedro asked.

The man set his pitchfork against the side of the barn and acted like he was thinking things over. "O.K. O.K. Might be I still have a few big mules out back that might serve your purpose. Young ones, too."

McCallum handed the money to Pedro. He turned to the stableman and nodded. "Fine. Pedro will pick out the two we want and pay you a fair price. A good but fair price, if you catch my drift. Don't even bother trying to shine him. Pedro knows more horse-trading tricks than I know ways to break a man's ribs while making it look like an accident."

The man gulped when he looked at McCallum. "Thought never crossed my mind otherwise," he said quietly.

"Good. Pedro, I'll head over to the general store and get us loaded up."

Pedro disappeared into the barn with the liveryman and Thad turned back toward the main street. He found what he was looking for a few doors down, two buildings right next to each other. One held a hardware and farm supply store while the other was a store that sold small sundries.

Within the hour, Thad had purchased pack

saddles, halters, bridles, blankets, extra canteens, ammunition, and enough foodstuffs to feed the two of them, if sparingly, for about a month on the trail. He wasn't a bit surprised that the prices seemed about twenty percent higher than normal.

When the Army goes on a spending spree, local merchants usually act like sharks in bloody water, and it's the locals that end up being bled out. For a moment, Thad actually reconsidered whether his friendship with Al was worth all this. He shook the thought from his head. He owed Al far too much. Besides, he had given his word, and that was something he would never go back on. Although it had not been on his list, McCallum bought a pair of field glasses that he felt might come in handy.

"Looks like the Army's not the only one going to war," the storekeeper joked.

"Just going on a hunting trip is all," McCallum explained. He was becoming annoyed with the salesman. There used to be a time when people in the West minded their own business. Whatever a man did, where he did it, and why he did it were his own concerns, not that of strangers.

"Awful lot of ammo for a hunting trip," the man remarked. He was obviously the curious type.

"Depends on what you're hunting, I suppose," McCallum answered abruptly. Before he left the store, he ordered his supplies delivered to the livery stable.

Once back out on the street, Thad met up with Pedro. He was carrying McCallum's Winchester along with his own rifle, a Springfield caliber .45-70 trap-door carbine. He handed over the Winchester.

"What about our horses?" Thad asked.

"They are already over at the stable, *jefe*," Pedro explained. "We got two good mules, and our horses will be stabled overnight as part of the deal."

"The mules look all right to you?"

"*Sí*, and the man, he knows they better stay that way," Pedro said, smiling.

"Good. Let's go find us some place to stay. Some place with a bath. I suspect it may be a while before we'll have a chance to have another one."

The two went off in search of a decent hotel. Fortunately, they didn't have very far to look. In towns like Columbus the hotels were usually the larger buildings. The sign on top of this one said Galloway Hotel. When they entered, McCallum immediately noticed that, although not new, it was clean and well maintained.

The hotel must have been considered opulent when it first opened. A large circular sofa was set in the center of the lobby directly under a big chandelier. The sofa was covered in red velvet. It would have cost a pretty penny just to have it shipped in, Thad thought as they approached the front desk.

He tapped the bell located on the front counter. A large, overweight, middle-aged man emerged from a room in back. The clerk was trying to cover his thinning hair by combing it across the top of his head, but in Thad's opinion it didn't work as planned. The fellow wore a black bowtie and a slightly stained white shirt with a high starched collar.

"Can I help you?" he asked, at the same time casting a rather nasty look over at Pedro.

"We need two rooms, if available, or, if not, make it one large room with two separate beds," McCallum explained. The look on the man's face had not been lost on him.

"Sorry, but we ain't allowing no greasers to stay here no more," the clerk commented rudely.

McCallum removed his pistol from its holster. He began inspecting the cylinder and, while still looking down at his gun, spoke to the clerk: "I see how it is. So, let me explain what's going to happen." He looked up at the clerk. "My pistol is going to accidentally go off and shoot you in the leg. Won't kill you, mind you, but it will hurt like hell, and you may be left with a permanent limp. You're then going to scream a lot and finally someone will call the sheriff."

"What?" the clerk said, shocked. His voice cracked and his expression was one of fear.

"Then the sheriff and I are going to have a talk. I'm going to explain to him that I am a personal friend of General Pershing's . . . which, by the way, I really am . . . and that this man is my friend, Pedro by name. He is also an American citizen. Then I am going to tell the sheriff to go check with the general and ask him about the man who shoved his ass into a ditch on Kettle Hill just as a Cuban fired a shot at him with a Mauser.

"General Pershing is going to reply that any man who had saved his life couldn't possibly be a liar, and that if you had been hit, it had to have come from an accidental discharge, like I said. Then the general will tell the sheriff in no uncertain terms not to bother with such petty things in the middle of a war zone.

"Next, the sheriff will let us go and we will end up right back here in the rooms you should have given us in the first place. Meanwhile, you will be in pain while we are resting comfortably in our hotel beds. Get the picture now?" McCallum spun the pistol's cylinder just to emphasize his point.

The clerk nodded slowly. His eyes never left the pistol.

McCallum cocked the Colt. "Well? Are there any rooms for both of us or not?"

The man nodded very quickly. "Yes, sir. As it happens I do have an unexpected opening, and I recall now that changes have been made in our policy regarding guests. It is a single room, but there are two beds in it. Very nice, I assure you."

"And the baths are on the same floor?" McCallum asked.

"Yes, sir," the clerk replied nervously. "And hot water, too."

McCallum nodded and reholstered his pistol. "Fine. We'll take the room." He smiled broadly. "Now, where do we sign in?"

The man turned the hotel book around for them to register, and as the clerk bent over, Pedro suddenly ran his finger over the top of the clerk's head. Then he made a face as he looked at his finger. "Very greasy, *jefe*."

McCallum nodded back at him. "Must be the food here," he replied.

Chapter Ten

Jeff Shaw finally had no choice. He had made as many excuses as he could and now he had to make the camera's magic happen. He would have to take pictures, and he knew they had better be good ones. After all, he was supposed to be a professional photographer.

Jeff was positioned behind the camera's tripod in an open field near a small herd of goats. All he knew for sure was that he was somewhere in northern Mexico. Back in Columbus, Jeff had been told that Chihuahua was the name of the Mexican state closest to New Mexico. What he didn't know was that it was the largest of the country's states. Considering how far they had traveled, Jeff had no idea if they were still in Chihuahua or whether they had crossed into some other state.

He did know one thing, however. Given the miles of open dry terrain, anyone unfamiliar with the country would be tracked down in no time whatsoever. So far, all Jeff had seen were miles and miles of open terrain with nothing but the occasional scrub tree, cactus, or small stream. There were mountains visible off in the distance, but without a map that fact was of no help to him.

After Albert Shaw, Jeff's father, had left the

military, he had spent most of his time growing his business in the city. As a child, Jeff had little opportunity to go camping, and his father never seemed to have the time to teach him things beyond the basics, like shooting.

If his father were in the same position, with his military background, he would escape and know how to survive and live off the land. But Jeff knew for certain, *he* couldn't, not without help. He simply didn't have his father's survival skills.

When you have nowhere to run, are surrounded by dangerous and angry men, and you value your life, you go along to get along. Jeff was determined to do just that. The problem was how to go along, get along, and still survive.

In front of him were ten men posing with their weaponry—pistols, swords, machetes, and rifles. Jeff had arranged the men in two lines with those who were tallest in back. Of course, out of respect, he had positioned General Villa in the middle, about two paces ahead of the rest. A place of honor.

Villa was wearing his small round sombrero, a black waistcoat, black pants, a white shirt, and a small tie. He wore bandoleers crossed over his chest like sashes and had two large Remington pistols stuck, cross-draw style, in his waistband.

Jeff lifted the cloth that was located at the rear of the camera and glanced through the front lens.

Objective was the description he remembered his uncle using. He reached around and removed the lens cap from the front of the camera. He then centered the image of the men in the camera's field of view. He knew that they were supposed to be upside down in this camera's viewer.

Also, he remembered his Uncle Jacob explaining that the older models required removing the lens cap for extended periods to expose the film plate and then replacing it, but this newer model had a cord with a sort of trigger on it. All you had to do was put the film in, remove the lens cover when you were ready, and push down on the cord's trigger to take the picture.

Jeff fumbled with the film cassette, initially trying to put it in upside down, but then he finally managed to load the camera properly. He held up the tray he had loaded with flash powder as he had seen his uncle do. It was sort of a metal stick with a pan on top. Jeff had to guess how much powder to use.

"O.K., gentleman, er . . . *caballeros*," he said, correcting himself. He couldn't bring himself to ask them to say cheese, so he simply said— "*Fuego*."—which he had been taught was Spanish for fire, and pushed the trigger on the cord.

The flash of smoke that went off was much louder and brighter than he had anticipated and when coupled with the word fire, it must have scared some of the men because they leveled their firearms and pointed them at Jeff.

"*¡Bueno! ¡Bueno!*" he yelled in Spanish. "It's all right, don't shoot!" he repeated in English. "Mercedes, for Christ's sake, tell them it's supposed to do that," he pleaded.

"*Está bien, muchachos,*" she said in Spanish. "*¡No disparen cobardes!*"

Jeff recognized the last word *cobardes*, as meaning cowards. He prayed the men would listen to her and wouldn't shoot him.

When Villa suddenly started laughing, most of the men relaxed. None of them wanted to be thought of as a weakling and very quickly they started laughing right along with him.

Jeff wiped his brow with the camera's drape and blew out a sigh of relief through his mouth. He had survived the first part of his problem, but the hardest part was still to come. He had to get the chemical processing just right for the film to develop into a picture. He had, however, thought ahead and had a plan. Good or bad, for the moment it was all he had.

"*¿Y la foto?*" Villa finally asked. Mercedes started to translate, but Jeff stopped her.

"I got it. I understand. Tell him that to develop the film, *la pelicula*, I need a place that is dark, or else the light will spoil the process."

Mercedes looked at him suspiciously but translated for General Villa.

"Tell him when we get to a village . . . if I can go inside somewhere . . . I can make the picture come out."

General Villa looked annoyed but nodded his understanding.

"For your sake, it better come out," Mercedes commented.

Jeff smiled at her. "I'm glad you're beginning to worry some about my safety. Means you care."

Mercedes stared at him and Jeff thought he detected a small smile trying to break through on her face. "No. I worry about the pictures *mi general* wants."

Chapter Eleven

The following morning, after grabbing a quick breakfast of tortillas wrapped around some eggs mixed with a spicy sausage called *chorizo*, Pedro rounded up the horses and packed the mules while Thad tried to locate a map of Mexico. Most of the more detailed ones had already been snatched up by the Army, but the general store in town still had one or two old ones left over.

McCallum didn't care much about how detailed the map was or how many names on the map might have been changed over the years. He just wanted to know where the main rivers, mountains, and towns were.

Pedro had grown up in these parts and probably knew northern Mexico better than any map maker, but since McCallum couldn't predict the future, he figured it was a good idea to have a little extra insurance in case a serious problem arose.

The two men met in front of the hotel, mounted up, and rode south. The river dividing Mexico and the United States might be the only one in the world with two names for the same place. Entering the American side, it was the Río Grande, but halfway across it became known by the Mexicans as the Río Bravo. The river is just as wet and muddy either way, but fortunately Pedro Peralta had found a relatively shallow place to ford, and they were soon across and into what Pedro referred to as *mi patria linda*, which McCallum knew translates to my beautiful homeland.

Thad recognized the emotions his friend must have felt when crossing back into the country where he was born, but he kept to himself his opinions as to the beauty of the place. As far as McCallum was concerned, the countryside here was just as flat, hot, and dusty as it was on the New Mexico side. As they loped along, he hoped that Pedro's description would materialize as they traveled farther south into the country.

After about four hours of riding the two men dismounted, loosened their saddle cinches, and then walked the horses for about twenty minutes. It was a habit McCallum had picked up in the Army, one that he still practiced to this day.

As they walked along, the men searched the horizon for any sign of activity. It was then that they saw several riders approaching.

Pedro raised his hand to cut the sun's glare and study the approaching men. *"Federales,"* he announced. McCallum had already guessed it.

There were four border guards and an officer. The men all wore high-pointed sombreros with a number five on them. McCallum assumed it was their unit's designation. The Mexicans pulled their horses to a halt, blocking their path.

"What are you doing crossing into our country, *señores*?" the officer asked in Spanish.

Pedro glared back at him. "It is also the country of my parents, my grandparents, and my great grandparents, *Capitán*."

The officer looked visibly upset. "It is *teniente*, not *capitán*. Again, I repeat, what are you doing crossing the *Río Bravo*?"

"Minding our own business," Pedro replied calmly.

Thad kept his mouth shut and let Pedro do all the talking. Although he understood quite a bit of Spanish, he didn't speak it well enough to get into a verbal confrontation. He merely continued to puff away on his pipe and listen.

"Since we are assigned this area to guard, it now becomes our business, too," the lieutenant explained. "So again, I ask you . . . what is your business here?"

"We are on our way south to visit the ranch of a distant relative who raises horses. *Señor* McCallum, here"—he threw his thumb in McCallum's direction—"is a horse trader and wishes to purchase some original Andalusian stock."

Thad smiled at the lieutenant.

The lieutenant looked skeptical. "And your name is?"

"I am Pedro Peralta, *Teniente*," he replied. "And as I said, this is *Señor* Thaddeus McCallum."

"And what is the name of this wealthy rancher relative of yours?" the officer asked. "The one you go to visit?"

Although he was careful not to show it, Pedro was stumped for a moment. He had not been anticipating that question. "His name is . . . *Don Quixote de la Mancha*," he answered calmly, and with a straight face.

Thad was so surprised, it was all he could do to keep from spitting out his pipe. He prayed silently that the Mexican officer was not a very literate man.

"*¿Quixote?*" The officer pushed his sombrero back. "It seems to me I have heard this name before."

"*Oh, sí, Teniente,* I am sure you have. My great uncle is very well known down south."

"How so?" the officer asked.

McCallum rolled his eyes to the sky and bit down hard on his pipe stem.

"Well, for one thing he was the one who discovered the famous lost golden helmet of Mambrino."

"Golden Helmet of Mambrino?" the lieutenant repeated dumbly.

Pedro simply nodded. "*Sí.* You know the one. I think it is now in the Chapultepec Museum in Mexico City. I hear he donated it to them."

The officer stared back at Pedro, nodding. Fortunately, he was the type of man who is too embarrassed to let others know he is ignorant on a subject, so he pretended he knew what Pedro was talking about. "*Sí*, that must be it. Certainly, that must be where I heard the name. And now he raises horses, you say?"

"*Teniente*, do you speak any English?" Thad asked, interrupting the conversation."

"*Sí, un poco*. A little," he replied. The word sounded like "leetle".

"We come in peace and mean no harm to anyone, I assure you. There are no weapons in our packs except for what is needed on the long trail. Now, I ask you, is there any way we can make you and your men more . . . shall we say . . . comfortable with our presence in your country?"

McCallum had lived long enough and had been around enough to know the code for making a financial offer without it sounding like a bribe.

"I know you and your men have come a long way and work hard, but now we all need to get on with our jobs," he added.

"*Sí*, that is true," the Mexican replied.

McCallum took out a wallet. While traveling he always carried two in case of robbery. The one he kept hidden carried a substantial stash of cash, while the other, which he brought out on occasions such as this, consisted of a much smaller sum, which he replenished as he went along.

"Now it isn't that we have a lot of money," he assured the lieutenant, "but this should take care of things and set your mind to rest that we are harmless. Wouldn't you agree, *Teniente*?"

Pedro confided in almost in a whisper. "*Jefe* has always been a generous man."

The officer looked back at his men uncomfortably, but nodded and winked at McCallum. He quickly took the folded cash McCallum was holding out.

"*Vaya con Dios, mi Teniente*," Pedro said in farewell.

"*Adiós*," the officer replied. He turned back to his men. "*Vamos, muchachos*. There is nothing more here."

With that the men turned and rode away, heading to the nearest town, McCallum guessed, where the money would make its way into the hand of some lucky *cantina* owner. When they were out of sight, McCallum let out a sigh of relief and turned to his friend.

"*Don* Quixote? Are you kidding me?" he said to Pedro. "You trying to get us killed on purpose?"

Pedro shrugged sheepishly. "It is my favorite book and I was reading it again before we left the ranch. It was all I could think of on the spur of the moment."

"Christ, Pedro, a million names in the damned

country and you come up with that one. Good thing for us you didn't claim we was visiting Benito Juarez or Hernán Cortés!"

Pedro shrugged. "But it worked, didn't it?"

Thad just shook his head. "Pedro, you always was the luckiest son-of-a-bitch I ever met. Golden Helmet of Mambrino, my ass." Then McCallum and Peralta both broke into raucous laughter.

"Well, *jefe*, any thoughts? Where do we go now?" Pedro asked after several minutes, wiping his brow with a large, red-checked kerchief.

"Hell, Pedro, it's your homeland. Your guess is as good as mine, and probably a damned sight better. So, what do you think? And for heaven's sake please don't just say south."

Pedro laughed, and then looked around for a moment or two while considering the options. "Southeast or southwest, *jefe*, your choice."

McCallum pushed his hat up and scanned the horizon again. "How am I supposed to know where they are?" he asked aloud.

"I don't know, either, but you got to think like Villa would, I guess."

"And how's that exactly?" Thad asked as his horse bobbed its head up and down, trying to flick a fly off its ear.

"Try to think like a *revolucionario, jefe*. Sooner or later Villa's going to want to hit a railroad train. If we ride diagonally from here, eventually we should cross some tracks," he reasoned.

McCallum nodded. "Makes sense. Trains carry all sorts of things that would be valuable to his army. Military trains carry supplies and weapons that he can't get in small towns, and trains are easier to attack than garrisons. Even civilian trains would be attractive. They'd be full of passengers loaded with money and jewelry that Villa can use to finance his activities."

"And General Pancho, he likes the publicity," Pedro added. "Robbing trains is always good for a page or two in the newspapers. It scares the hell out of people and the reporters, you know, they love that sort of thing."

"They sure do," Thad agreed. "So, what if we go east and he's heading west?" he asked more to himself than to Pedro.

"Then we wait until we hear something, or maybe we head in the other direction later," Peralta said, and smiled. "Either way we'll meet up with him soon enough, I think."

"Great," Thad mumbled, wondering what he'd gotten himself into. "You got a preference, my friend?"

Pedro just shook his head. "No, *jefe*."

"Good. Southeast it is then."

Both men lowered their hats, tightened their cinches, and headed out. It promised to be a long, hot, and dusty ride.

Chapter Twelve

Anyone else might have felt the days were passing with a certain degree of monotony. Jeff was far from feeling anything of the sort. Two things kept him from being bored. First there were the occasional moments of fear and terror, such as when Villa located a town or a government patrol to attack, or when the men got drunk and began shooting at everything and everyone in sight. The second factor was the constant companionship of his translator and instructor, Mercedes. Dangerous as Julio Cardenas was, Jeff still couldn't keep his eyes off her.

Jeff was a quick learner and had always had an aptitude for language and the arts, so it was no surprise that he was picking up Spanish quickly. Of course, he wasn't letting anyone else know that. Especially not Mercedes. The moment Villa thought he had learned to palaver well enough in their language, he would end Mercedes's lessons. And Jeff wanted as much time with her as possible. In fact, as is often the case with young men his age, fascination was quickly turning into love. To a degree, she was all he could think about, except perhaps for considering ways to help him survive or to escape.

Close proximity for long periods often creates a romantic effect on members of both sexes, and Mercedes was no exception. Of course, she was no stranger to romantic advances. No girl of her age with her looks would be. Surprisingly, however, she found Jeff Shaw somehow strangely different. The *Americano* always treated her with the utmost respect and with none of the usual *machismo* she was so accustomed to from the soldiers.

Mercedes couldn't help but realize that Jeff was nowhere nearly as possessive, jealous, or demanding as Julio was. Not by a long shot. For added measure it certainly didn't hurt that Jeff was a good-looking man in any girl's book.

While his inexperience and infatuation were clearly obvious to her, the more time she spent working with him, the more endearing those traits became. The only thing that surprised Mercedes was how such a bright and capable young man could be so slow and thick when it came to learning such a simple language. She often had to get close, roll her lips, and repeat even the simplest of words for him over and over.

Whenever General Villa stopped to make camp, Jeff practiced his photographic techniques. It was in a small village the he had developed successfully the photograph he had taken of Villa and his men. Villa had been pleased.

Jeff's confidence grew and he began taking more photos, and then developing them in the wagon in a makeshift darkroom he put together. So far, his best success had been a picture of Mercedes. She had insisted in posing with her holstered pistol, her rifle, and crossed bandoleers of bullets. Her hat was resting on her back, held in place by a thin strap. The wind was picking up as Jeff had focused on her head and shoulders, effectively cropping out the weapons.

The result was a portrait of a beautiful woman with her hair blowing in the wind. As soon as Mercedes saw it, she instantly realized how Jeff truly saw her. Not as a guerrilla soldier, or some *campesina*, but as a real woman. Even as hardened as she had become, Mercedes couldn't help but be touched.

The two of them were on the edge of the camp, talking and smiling at one another, when Julio Cardenas walked up behind her. Looking over her shoulder, he took note of the picture and grunted. Reaching over, he grabbed it right out of her hand and stuffed it in his shirt pocket.

"Hey!" Jeff yelled angrily. "Give that back."

Realizing the danger in which he was putting himself, Mercedes put her hand on Jeff's chest and pushed him back. "No! Leave it be."

"Like hell, I will," he replied, sticking out his hand toward Cardenas. "*La foto*, it's not yours."

Cardenas smiled wickedly, and then spit on

Jeff's extended hand. Al Shaw had tried to teach his son one important lesson about fighting: *Don't ever go looking for trouble, but when it finally comes and you have to hit someone, try to put them away with the first punch. Hit first and hit hard. You can't count on getting a second chance.*

Jeff remembered those words and proceeded to throw his best haymaker. He hit Cardenas squarely on the jaw with all his might. Julio stumbled back a step or two, but to Jeff's dismay, he didn't even come close to going down. If anything, he just looked meaner. Slowly the man pulled out a large, wicked-looking Bowie knife from his belt.

"Julio, no!" Mercedes pleaded.

Cardenas merely shoved her off to the side. Jeff had learned enough Spanish to understand what Cardenas was saying to her. Roughly it translated to: "I'm going to carve this damned *gringo* into little pieces like I should have done in the first place."

Shaw might have taught his son to box a little, but knife fighting was something totally different. Often, in a close match, both the winner and the loser end up with wounds to various, and sometimes numerous, parts of their body. In this case Cardenas was not only bigger, stronger, and more experienced, he was also the only one armed.

As much as Jeff wanted to run, he wouldn't. Certainly, not in front of the girl. As Cardenas started forward, Jeff desperately looked around for something to use for protection or as a weapon. He needed something to keep Cardenas at bay, be it a chair, a shovel, or anything with some weight to it. Quickly he spotted the camera's tripod. Fortunately, Jeff had already removed the camera, so he rushed over and snatched it up.

Jeff pushed the tripod out in front, fending off the angry soldier's arm, much like a lion tamer would use a stool or a chair to avoid getting clawed. The idea worked for a moment or two, but the difference is that lions don't grab and hang onto the chair.

After a couple of failed attempts to slash his opponent, Cardenas got smart. He feigned a thrust with his knife, and when Jeff parried his thrust, the movement pushed the tripod right into Julio's other hand. One strong pull was all it took to yank it free from Jeff's grip.

"*Ahora te mueras, gringo,*" he said, sneering wickedly.

Jeff knew what he meant. "Now you die."

Just as Cardenas prepared to attack, he heard a loud angry shout. At the sound of that voice Cardenas hesitated and glanced back over his shoulder.

"*No, Capitán Cardenas. ¡Dejalo! Es un orden,*"

General Villa shouted, ordering his man to stop.

Jeff was never so grateful for anything in his life. Cardenas on the other hand was furious.

"*Gracias, Mi General*," Jeff replied quickly, trying his best to stay on Villa's good side.

Cardenas started to explain something, but Villa merely held up his hand. He wasn't interested in details; he just wanted his photographer to remain in one piece. That much he made very clear to his second in command.

Cardenas was not satisfied, but he knew better than to argue with Villa, so he started to leave. He had only taken a few steps when Jeff suddenly told him to stop.

"He has my photograph," he explained nervously to the general.

"*¿Asi es? Julio, ven aca*," Villa said, indicating with a gesture of his hand that he wanted to see the picture. Once he saw it, he looked over at Mercedes and began to laugh loudly. "*Ahora entiendo*." Even though Jeff had understood Villa, the leader turned to him and said in English: "I understand."

Villa studied the two men for a moment, then he smiled, handing the small portrait back to Jeff. The look that followed in Julio Cardenas's eyes was something to remember and to fear.

Jeff nodded his head at Villa as he tucked the picture inside his shirt.

Mercedes shook her head and stormed off. She'd had enough of male egos for the day.

Again, General Villa ordered Cardenas to leave Jeff alone, but the lad knew that he would never be safe as long as that soldier was nearby.

Chapter Thirteen

Pancho Villa's men broke camp two days later, and the army headed out. Jeff had no clue as to what plans the general had made, but there was a distinct excitement in the air among his soldiers. At the same time, Jeff felt a palpable nervousness.

For almost a week the army moved due south. Although they had no way of knowing it, they were almost on a parallel track with the route McCallum and Peralta were taking. Finally, Villa ordered a halt in a stand of trees overlooking a valley. Jeff could see nothing except the valley floor and empty railroad tracks running across it.

Jeff was puzzled until he saw a small patrol ride down into the valley. He watched them as they stopped at the railroad tracks. From his location, he couldn't see exactly what they were doing at first, but, watching, it didn't take long for him to realize they were loosening the track.

Jeff addressed the next soldier to ride by his wagon. "A train is coming, right? Um ... *¿Viene un tren, verdad?*"

The soldier laughed and nodded his head. "*Sí. ¡Viva la revolución!*"

Jeff nodded back with an obvious lack of enthusiasm. As much as he tried over the next several hours to think of something to do, he knew it would be either futile or downright suicidal for him to try to do anything to warn the train.

General Villa had spelled out the plan to his officers. A rider had previously brought him information regarding a government shipment of guns and ammunition that was being shipped by train. It would be manned with federal troops riding the roof tops of the train cars and they would be equipped with several machine-guns.

Because of the machine-guns, Villa knew a straight, head-on attack on horseback would surely fail and result in a great loss of life among his army. One thing was certain about Francisco Villa—he was clever. He had spent the last several days waiting while a small group of his men had been scouting ahead, looking for just the right place for a surprise attack on the train. This was the location on the tracks they had felt to be most advantageous to their attack.

At one point during the night Cardenas rode past Jeff Shaw's wagon and ordered him tied up again. Jeff glared at him as the captain rode off. It had no effect on Villa's right-hand man, but, given the circumstances, it was the only way he could express his hatred. Jeff knew it was all he could do, short of getting himself killed on the spot.

Julio Cardenas rode into the valley with fifty

men and scattered them on both sides of the tracks behind trees, rocks, and in gullies and ravines. He let his men know that if any of them were spotted, the whole unit would suffer, and not just from the guns of the *federales*.

Their horses were led away by ten of the soldiers. The captain scouted around and was satisfied that when viewed from the direction the train would be coming, the entrance to the valley looked like a peaceful, empty stretch of land.

Villa was betting that after an uneventful night riding the tops of the railcars without a rest, the soldiers would be tired and not paying that much attention to the land around them.

The best thirty marksmen in Villa's army were positioned higher up the valley wall, approximately five hundred yards from the tracks. Fifteen of them were stationed hidden on either side of the tracks. Those on the valley wall would practically be shooting level with the train car tops.

From his vantage point Jeff could only sit and watch. He was perched on his wagon seat, arms and legs securely tied. Given the time it was taking to prepare for the attack, Jeff figured the supply train would be passing through the area at an early hour. Even though it would be unlikely that he could be heard at that distance, a bandanna had been tied around his mouth to ensure he would not attempt to warn the train. To

Jeff it seemed that Captain Cardenas's orders had been carried out to an extreme by the soldiers, who seemed more afraid of the captain than of the upcoming battle.

Jeff had no watch, but when he heard the train enter the valley, he guessed it was around 5:00 or 6:00 in the morning. The train was running fast, making good time, but the early morning fog in the valley and the dim light of dawn made it almost impossible for the engineer to see that the tracks had been altered.

The engine hit the gap that had been created by loosening the pins and shifting the rails at full speed. The first five cars veered off the tracks, which sent the following cars swerving, tilting, and, in some cases, turning over, which resulted in the end section of the train fish-tailing. *Federales* were thrown from the top of the train upon impact and many inside were slammed into the walls. Almost immediately the *revolucionarios* began firing from their hiding places.

Villa waited almost a full ten minutes for his marksmen and other shooters to battle against the guns firing back from the train. Then, with a mighty yell, the rest of his men charged on horseback from the opposite end of the valley.

Jeff watched in horror as men hacked at the *federales* with their machetes and gunned down the government soldiers who attempted to escape.

He had assumed that any civilian found on the train would be treated as a non-combatant. After all, General Villa professed to be a liberator, and therefore civilians should be treated accordingly. Jeff was shocked to learn that this was not to be the case.

Atop his wagon, Jeff had a clear view of the attack. As men, women, and children spilled from the train's compartments, they were gunned down. It was a bloody massacre.

Jeff watched helplessly for almost two hours as bodies were searched and stripped of personal possessions. Wagons were brought in and the train was emptied of boxes of supplies. Finally, when the shooting and the screaming were over, the silence gave way to loud shouts of victory. Over and over the *Villaistas* in the valley shouted: "¡*Viva Villa, Viva Méjeco!*" and "¡*Viva la Revolución!*" They were joyful and triumphant while Jeff Shaw was feeling sick to his stomach at what he had just witnessed, and fearing he would have to document with photographs this massacre later in the morning.

Chapter Fourteen

Thad and Pedro had been riding southeast for a couple of weeks without encountering anything more than the occasional sheep or goat herder.

"I don't know how I could do that day after day," Thad remarked after they rode by a solitary herder sitting on a small hill. There was no other sign of life as far as the eye could see.

"Why not, *jefe*?" Pedro asked. Even as they chatted neither of the two ever stopped scanning the horizon, looking for potential signs of danger as they traveled farther south.

"Oh, I reckon I'd go plumb loco from boredom just sitting there day in, day out. What do those herders even think about out here"—he made a sweeping motion with his hand—"in the middle of nowhere?"

"They think small, *jefe*," Pedro replied.

"Small? Whatcha mean? Think small?"

"Well, *jefe*, you always think big. You know, managing the ranch, growing the herd, and now how to save this boy for your friend. Big things. But these *campesinos*, they just think small."

"How so?" Thad asked. "I'm not sure I catch your drift."

"Well, they have more time to do nothing, so they notice the things around them," Pedro went on. "Like how ants move before it rains, or why one goat jumps one way while another always jumps the other way. Small things."

"I guess I get it," Thad replied, even though it was hard for him to comprehend. "If you don't have anything to worry about, there's nothing much to think about, right?"

"Sort of like that, *jefe*," Pedro replied, nodding. "But I think it is more like they just live in the moment and don't think much about the past or future."

Thad chuckled. "Maybe I could do with a little more of that kind of attitude."

Pedro shook his head. "No, *jefe*, I think not. Then you wouldn't be you."

Switching the reins to his left hand, McCallum pulled out his pipe from its pouch and filled its bowl with tobacco. Then he struck a match on one of the saddle *conchos* and lit the pipe.

"Maybe you're right, Pedro," he said, puffing a cloud of smoke. "But then again, maybe that wouldn't be so bad?" They both laughed as they rode along.

The next day Thad could feel that the black's gait was different somehow. The horse was bobbing his head more, and as Thad rode, he felt his weight being shifted off to the side.

"Hey, Pedro, ride up alongside and check out the black's gait for me, would you?"

"*Sí, jefe*. I can tell you already from here I can see he is favoring his right front leg. I have been watching for the last couple of miles," Pedro replied.

Thad shrugged and pulled to a halt. "Might as well have a look."

The men dismounted, and McCallum handed his friend the reins. He proceeded to lift the black's leg, and then checked the shoe. There is an old saying: *No foot, no horse.* On the trail a lame horse is almost as good as no horse.

Thad reached into his pocket and pulled out a special pocket knife that also housed a hoof pick in addition to two blades. He used the hook to clean the dirt off from around the inside of the horseshoe and the hoof's sole.

"Don't see any quarter cracks or embedded stones," Thad asked Pedro. "The horseshoe nails seem O.K. to me. Did you bring the hoof testers?"

Pedro looked at his friend as if disappointed. "You would ever doubt that, *jefe*? Of course, I did. They are in the lead mule's saddlebags."

Peralta walked the animals over to a nearby shrub and tied them off. He opened one of the saddlebags and removed a pair of flat-edged nippers and a hoof tester. He took McCallum's place at the horse's leg and, using the pliers and nippers, removed the shoe and nails and cleaned the hoof underneath.

A hoof tester looks sort of like a pair of ice tongs, but, instead of having pick-like tips, they have small rounded ends. Pedro began to work carefully around the hoof, gently squeezing with the tester. Occasionally he would stop to clean and trim any excess hoof growth using a sharp, curved hoof trimmer.

"We got lucky this time, *jefe*. I think it is just a stone bruise," Pedro concluded.

McCallum put his hand to his mouth and pulled out his pipe. He glanced around the area, checking for anything that looked out of place. He then used the pipe stem to point, gesturing at the hoof. "Still, even with a bruise he's lame. What we need is a set of shoes with higher heels to keep his hoof off the ground till that bruise heals. And I know you don't have a set of those in your bag."

"Sorry, *jefe*. No can do." Pedro shrugged sadly.

"Well, we still have a distance to go and I don't want to ruin him. Any ideas?"

Pedro thought for a moment. "We might be able to pad it with something to keep the bruise from making contact with the ground."

"The question is how. You think wrapping the whole hoof with something might work?"

Peralta shook his head. "Wouldn't be thick enough and he'd probably wear it right off. Let me think." He walked over to the mules and pulled off a leather saddlebag. He stared at it a moment, and then removed the contents from the bag on one side and shifted them into the other side. Then, using his pocket knife, he cut off the empty saddlebag's big flap.

"This should be thick enough, *jefe*. We put it under the sole and right over the horseshoe. The pressure from the shoe and the horseshoe nails will keep it in place. The leather pad, it should protect the sole against stones and help prevent any more pain, I think."

"At least until we can find a farrier to put on corrective shoes," Thad added, nodding his approval.

"Maybe there will be one in the next *pueblo*," Pedro replied.

"Hope so. I like this horse."

Pedro then set the leather flap on the ground under the horse's hoof. After tracing out the hoof's border, Pedro then cut part of the flap away. When he was finished nailing the thick piece of leather under the hoof, there was now a molded pad in place to protect the bottom of the horse's sole.

"That ought to do it, Pedro," McCallum observed. "Nice job."

"*Gracias, jefe*. But even so, we should take it slow until we get new shoes made, and maybe reshape the heels a mite."

McCallum remounted slowly. He shifted himself in the saddle and raised himself up and down, testing the black's reaction. When he was confident it was all right, he said: "Well, then we best get going. No sense in wasting more time."

Unfortunately, it was four more days before they finally rode into a small town. This one was called Los Potros. It was a toss-up as to who or what was dustier, the horses, the men, or the town. Los Potros was five blocks long and, with the exception of a small plaza that was circled by a cobblestone walkway, there wasn't much to recommend the place.

Such plazas were supposed to be the center of activity and they were always well cared for. Many even had a good deal of decorative stonework. It seemed to McCallum that almost every town he'd seen south of the border had such a town square, which, as far as he could tell, was only used on Sundays when the town's young men and *señoritas* congregated, passing the time by walking around in circles. Thad guessed this was some part of the courting ritual, but it didn't make any sense to him. In fact, he wondered why the young men even showed up since the *señoritas* were always accompanied by their *chaperones*. And the *chaperónes* were always elderly females, probably relatives, whose dour expressions could peel bark from a tree.

Apparently, they were there to keep the men away and protect the honor of the girls. The few *chaperónes* he'd seen would have come in handy going up Kettle Hill—they'd have scared the pants right off the enemy.

The two riders pulled up to a small water trough and dismounted. They let their horses and pack mules drink their fill before tying them to a nearby hitching post. Both men removed their hats, dipped their kerchiefs in the water, and wiped their faces and hair free of dust and dirt as best they could.

As he was shaking the water out of his hair, McCallum saw three men talking to each other at the end of the street. He couldn't help but notice that the trio seemed to be glancing in his and Pedro's direction.

Nudging his partner, Thad whispered to Pedro: "Don't be too obvious but check out those three to your right. They seem just a mite too interested in our livestock."

Pedro casually put his kerchief and sombrero back on as he sneaked glances at the group. Before he could form any sort of impression, however, the three men turned, mounted their nearby horses, and rode out of town.

"*Revolucionarios* maybe?" Thad asked. "Think they could be from the group we're looking for, Pedro?"

"I don't know, *jefe*," he replied, shrugging.

Peralta adjusted his hat. "Could be. On the other hand, maybe they're just simple *vaqueros* working for a nearby *hacienda*."

McCallum shook his head. "I don't know. They spent an awful lot of time checking us out."

"Well, it's not every day a tall *gringo* rides into a place like this," Pedro noted. "Could be they're just curious about you. Anyway, they're gone now."

Thad took a piece of licorice out of his pocket and popped it in his mouth. "Guess you're right. Maybe I'm just overly cautious, but something about them made the hair on the back of my neck stand up."

"You worry too much, *jefe*," Pedro chuckled. "Better to save what little hair you have left, I think."

"Wise ass," McCallum replied, squinting his eyes in mock anger.

"Come on, *jefe*. They're gone now. Stop worrying. What say we go into that *cantina* and wet our whistles?"

Thad glanced around. "Might as well. Let's get something to eat, too. I don't think there's anything else to do here. It's not Sunday and, even if it was, I don't feel much like walking in circles."

Pedro frowned. Sometimes his *jefe* said some rather strange things that he didn't understand.

La Cabrita was a typical small town *cantina*. It

had a half a dozen or so tables scattered around a small room with a slatted wood floor. There was a long, curved bar at the far end directly across from the door. Half of the bar was dedicated to selling bottles of mescal, tequila, or home-made beer, while the other half served as a makeshift kitchen complete with clay pots filled with refried beans, rice, and boiled chicken. On the floor behind the bar was a small tortilla oven with a chimney that ran up the wall and out the roof.

Despite the humble nature of the town, the *cantina* was very clean and filled with wonderful aromas. There were the usual hand-painted pictures representing the local landscape and several old guitars hanging on the walls at different angles.

The two chose a table that was positioned by the wall, giving them a clear view of the room while protecting their backs. A rather plump matron waited on them. Pedro ordered two beers, chicken and rice soup, and some tortillas. The food was served with slices of lemon that were meant to be squeezed into the soup and over pieces of chicken. Thad never did understand the fascination with lemon the people south of the border all seemed to have. They squeezed it over meat, in their soups, with shots of tequila, and even put it on the rims of beer mugs, along with a layer of salt. Personally, he preferred doing without it.

On the table were three small bowls filled with hot sauce. One was red with spicy chili pepper granules in it, the other was similar, but green and much hotter, and the third contained something Pedro called *mole*. He pronounced it "molay" and it tasted sort of like spicy chocolate.

McCallum could never understand why ketchup had never caught on in Mexico. Hell, they certainly had enough tomatoes on hand and in his opinion ketchup was a lot tastier. More importantly it didn't aggravate his dyspepsia. Back in the States, Thad put ketchup on just about everything he ate. One time, he almost got booted out of a friend's Thanksgiving dinner after requesting ketchup for his turkey and dressing. He was lucky the fellow's wife hadn't hauled into him with the carving knife she had in her hand.

Halfway through their meal in the *cantina* McCallum brought up the issue of the *Villaistas*. "Shouldn't we ask around and see if anyone knows the whereabouts of this Pancho Villa?"

At the sound of Villa's name, the bartender put down a bottle rather loudly and several patrons turned to look at the two strangers.

Pedro put a finger to his lips to indicate caution. "Remember, *jefe*, not all the people in these small towns are on his side. We don't want to raise any unnecessary suspicion until we understand who and what we are dealing with. People in such towns like this, they are usually wary of everyone. The government, revolutionaries, strangers . . . everyone."

"You think spreading some money around town might help?" McCallum asked.

"That depends, *jefe*. It might if they have no connection to the general. But if they are on his side and suspect we are here to do him harm, or if they think we are working for the government, *dinero* or no, they would kill us without hesitation."

"Can't we just explain we're looking for a friend?" Thad asked.

"Sure, if they believe us. If they don't, we might never see our ranch again," Pedro said, shaking his head.

"So, what do you reckon we should do?"

"Finish our lunch. Then I will ask around town by myself. If the wrong people hear a tall *gringo* mentioning *that* name again, well, maybe we don't even get to finish this splendid feast," Pedro said, waving his hand over the dishes of food on the table.

McCallum nodded solemnly in agreement and took another spoonful of the soup. "Fine with me. Just be careful about who and how you ask."

Pedro put some chicken into a tortilla and rolled it up. "Oh, trust me, *jefe*, I will."

"While we're at it, maybe we can track down a decent farrier."

Chapter Fifteen

That evening Jeff Shaw went looking for Mercedes. Jeff knew it was a foolish thing to do, for if Julio Cardenas even suspected his intent, he would die a quick death despite the general's warnings to his right-hand man. But Jeff Shaw was a young man in love and simply couldn't help himself.

No longer closely guarded during the day, Jeff was allowed to wander somewhat freely around the camp. After all, there was no point in keeping him tied up. Villa just made sure Jeff was not allowed access to the horses or weapons. Still, even if he did escape, his odds of success were slim to none. Jeff had been repeatedly informed that a *gringo* would stand out like a sore thumb in this region, and he had been led to believe that all the people in the region were *Villaistas* at heart. Jeff did his best not to bother the men, and Villa's men, seeing how the general seemed to favor this *gringo*, basically left him alone.

Jeff found Mercedes leaning against a tree on the outskirts of the camp. She seemed to be lost in thought. Back in the center of camp a few of the men had begun playing guitars and the music drifted in the air.

Mercedes gasped slightly when Jeff approached.

He in turn thought that he had never seen anything as beautiful as the vision of this woman with the stars shining above her.

"What are you doing here? Are you crazy?" she exclaimed. "If Julio finds you are here alone with me, he will kill us both."

Jeff smiled at her. "Guess so, but it's crazy to be in love," he whispered. "There I said it. I can't help it. I've fallen in love with you and don't care who knows."

Mercedes shook her head. "You're just young and away from home. Maybe you got a hold of some locoweed. You should go."

Jeff took a step closer and put his hands on her shoulders. He felt her shudder as he looked into her eyes. Gathering up his courage, he pulled her to him and gave her a long kiss.

Instead of pulling away, Mercedes relaxed into his arms. When he stopped, she raised her hand up as if to slap him, but then dropped it in surrender. Jeff kissed her again. "Still want me to go?" he asked softly.

Mercedes smiled and put a finger to his lips. "*Sí*, I want you to go, but only for your own safety. Julio will be looking for me and he must not see you here."

The thought of Julio being near her filled him with a burning hatred.

"I can't stand the thought of that animal being around you," Jeff hissed.

"You must go. Don't worry I will think of some way to get you to safety," she explained.

"Know this, I'm not going anywhere without you, not now, not ever," Jeff said.

Mercedes leaned in and gave him a kiss before shoving Jeff back toward camp. "Go now."

Jeff went reluctantly, but when he glanced back, she was still looking his way. He now knew she cared about him, too. Of that he was sure. What he didn't know was that she was wondering what in the world she had gotten herself into and why she had ever allowed herself to fall in love. And with a *gringo*!

Chapter Sixteen

After their meal, Thad and Pedro split up. Thad made a big show of checking the horses and mules, adjusting their saddles and packs to stall for time. Pedro wandered into the general store on the pretext of buying tobacco and some canned goods for the trail.

Everyone knows there are three places to pick up local gossip. One is the town saloon or *cantina*, another is the town barbershop, and the last one is the shebang or general store. After explaining how he came to be riding with an *Americano*, sticking with the story that he was helping him acquire horses, Pedro eventually learned that Villa's men hadn't been seen in this town for over a year.

"Well, any news?" Thad asked when his friend returned.

"There are rumors that a couple of weeks back Villa's men fought the American army at Nogales," Pedro replied.

"How'd it go?" Thad asked his friend.

"Half the town thinks Villa won and the other half thinks he lost. Villa is supposed to be operating to the southwest of us, maybe on the way to the city of Chihuahua. But it's all rumor. Some think he might head east."

"So, we split the difference and ride south," McCallum said more to himself than to his friend. "What about the three men who were eyeballing us?" he asked.

"No one knows. They're not from around here. Probably just riding through looking for work." Pedro put tobacco, rice, and a couple of cans of peaches in one of the saddlebags, and then mounted his horse. "Good news is, there is a blacksmith at the far end of town," he added.

Before mounting, Thad stretched his back and groaned.

"You all right, *jefe*?" Pedro asked, concerned.

Thad moved a small barrel close to his horse and used it as a step.

"Nothing losing twenty years wouldn't fix. Apparently, I'm as all right as I'm gonna be at my age. Damned rheumatism kicks in now and then is all. I'm fine, so stop acting like an old lady and let's go find the damned farrier."

Peralta knew by now not to argue when his boss was in one of his moods, so he just nodded and put a soft spur to his mount.

At the end of the *pueblo* the two men found the local blacksmith. He was a short, bearded man with bare arms the size of tree trunks. He wore a leather apron and had a gray towel stuffed into his back pocket that hung halfway down his leg.

Pedro explained the problem as the farrier got

right to work, lifting the black's hoof. He smiled and shook his head. Thad knew enough Spanish to recognize the compliment the man was paying Pedro for the fix he'd made.

"*Necesito mas o menos una hora,*" the man said, explaining it would take an hour to perform the necessary work.

"Might as well hang out here," McCallum said, sitting down on a nearby chair that had been made from a large, cut-down rain barrel. He took out his tobacco pouch and filled his pipe.

Pedro chatted casually with the blacksmith who was named Alfredo. He had learned the trade from his father and had lived his whole life in the same town. Once he determined the blacksmith had no information that could be of any use to them, Pedro left him to his work and sat down next to Thad and rolled a cigarette.

When Alfredo finished his work, he told the two men he thought there would be little danger in riding the black with the pad and the new shoes he'd fashioned. They had a slight lift and he had shaped the hoof to keep the sole off the ground and protected.

Both Thad and Pedro agreed the man had done a great job. The horseshoe nails were well seated and everything was trimmed smooth. Thad gladly paid the man's asking price and tossed in a good tip.

Then they mounted and were ready to ride. Out of habit both men looked back as they left town, making sure they weren't being followed.

Five hours later the two men were riding through a small but deep gully. As they rounded the bend of the relatively narrow passage, they found themselves facing a group of six mounted Mexicans. Three of the men were the ones McCallum had spotted back in town.

Neither Thad nor Peralta took their eyes off the group as they reined in their mounts.

"Revolutionaries? They with Villa?" Thad whispered.

Peralta looked them over and shook his head. "*Bandidos*," he whispered, undoing his holster's restraint thong from off his pistol.

"*Buenos días, caballeros*," one of the men said, greeting them.

"*Buenos días*," Pedro replied. "We'd like to pass through, if you don't mind," he said in Spanish. Thad subtly patted his holster to make sure his gun was free.

The three men they had seen in town shook their heads, smirking.

"Not without paying for passage," the man closest to McCallum declared to Pedro. He presented himself as the group's leader.

"He says we have to pay to go through, *jefe*," Peralta translated out of the corner of his mouth.

Thad nodded his head. "Uhn-huh. I know. Ask him what his price is. How much?"

Pedro hadn't taken his eyes off the group. "*¿Cuanto?*" he asked.

The leader, not one of the three from town, looked back and forth between the two men facing him.

"Why are you riding with a *gringo*?" he asked Pedro.

Pedro looked annoyed and, ignoring him, merely repeated his question. "*¿Cuanto?*"

The bandit smiled and rubbed his chin. He was a short, stocky man with a short unkempt beard. He was wearing a dirty leather vest and had an old Colt in his holster which he wore cross-draw style.

"I'll tell you what, *muchacho*, you both can pass for the low price of your mules and horses. Then you can walk right on through." Several of the men snickered when they heard the price.

"*Jefe* . . . ," Pedro started to say.

"I got it already," McCallum replied angrily. "Tell him I need a moment to make a counter-offer," Thad said, moving his horse forward a step or two. He then stopped and, while Pedro translated, Thad slowly removed his riding gloves and tucked them into the left side of his belt. He then carefully pulled out his pipe and tobacco pouch.

"There are six of them, *jefe*," Pedro reminded him in almost a whisper.

"Uhn-huh," McCallum grunted. "Tell him he can have just one mule."

While Pedro began negotiations with the man, Thad began tamping down the tobacco in the pipe bowl. His gestures were slow and deliberate.

The Mexican leader began shouting, and the men shifted in their saddles.

"No good, *jefe*," Pedro said. "He says all or nothing, and that includes our weapons."

McCallum nudged his horse forward another step and stopped, facing the band's leader. "Pedro, tell him I need just a moment to think about his offer." Then the old trooper put his pipe in his mouth and bit down. He returned the tobacco pouch to his coat pocket, and then, with his right hand, reached slowly into his vest pocket. He pulled a match out with methodical care. Thad struck the match on his belt buckle and raised it to his pipe.

The outlaws appeared a little confused by his actions. They had expected the two men either to react angrily or surrender quickly. McCallum's request for a short delay to think had them both puzzled and a little curious.

Peralta had been in a similar situation with Thad once or twice before and quickly realized what his friend was up to. He shifted in his saddle to keep a better eye on the bandits.

Thad McCallum stared at the Mexican leader as he lowered the match to the pipe bowl. There was no wind blowing and the little gully was as quiet as a cemetery. Peralta hoped it wouldn't be his final resting place.

Thad held the match to the pipe bowl, puffing on the pipe for what seemed to be an eternity. He then lifted the burning match, his eyes never leaving the Mexican leader, and continued to puff, creating a halo of smoke around his head. It appeared as though he was so intent on making sure the bowl was lit properly that he had forgotten all about the match.

The outlaws were mesmerized by his actions as the flame worked its way down to the end of the match and burned his fingers.

The tension was broken when McCallum let out a loud yell: "Ouch! God dammit all to hell."

Several of the bandits started laughing as McCallum shook his hand up and down to cool his burned fingertips. His arm went up and down in an exaggerated and painful manner as he continued cursing. Down . . . up . . . down . . . and finally up.

When Thad's hand was on the upswing, it held his Colt pistol. McCallum began firing before anyone realized what was happening. Anyone except Pedro, that is.

At the same time McCallum had pulled his

gun, Pedro had drawn his. In unison, both began fanning their revolvers. Pedro went for the men on his right, while Thad was working his way over from the left.

The two friends were outgunned six to two, but they both carried six shot revolvers whereas two of the Mexicans were armed with single-shot rifles that they had been carrying muzzle down and partially across their saddles.

In any given situation action is usually quicker than reaction, something McCallum had learned long ago. The only way to counter this effect is to be the one to start the action in the first place. The outlaw group's leader had been taken by surprise and was the first one down, taking a .45-caliber slug from McCallum's Colt Peacemaker right in his throat.

Peralta's shots knocked down two men, and then as one of the bandits raised his rifle at him, Pedro threw himself from his saddle to get out of the line of fire. Rolling on the ground, he felt a shot stir up the dirt right next to him. Still rolling, Peralta returned fire on instinct. Out of the corner of his eye he saw his target drop his rifle and fall sideways from his horse.

Another outlaw was blown backward out of his saddle by McCallum's shooting, and once Pedro stood back up, he turned to face the remaining outlaw. The man fired at Pedro but, without enough time to aim, his shot missed.

The final two shots from McCallum and Peralta put the man down to stay.

"You O.K., Pedro?" Thad asked.

"*Sí, jefe*. But it was close."

"No choice to it. Out here without our livestock and packs we'd have been as good as dead anyway."

Pedro nodded in agreement. "Too bad, but better them than us."

"That's for sure, Pedro, that's for damned sure." McCallum removed his hat and wiped his brow with his kerchief. His pipe had not left his mouth during the fight.

"Should we break out the shovels and bury these men, *jefe*?" Pedro asked.

McCallum shrugged his shoulders. "Well, I suppose it is the God-fearing thing to do," he replied. "But we dig only one hole for these buzzards. They can all go to hell together. No way we're digging six separate graves. I'm getting too old for this horseshit."

Chapter Seventeen

By now Jeff had become quite proficient at taking and developing pictures and, except for the occasional encounter with Captain Julio Cardenas, he had begun almost to enjoy his adventure, especially his time with Mercedes. They had been riding for several days now, and Jeff was wondering if Villa had a destination in mind.

Riding with a rebel army that is supposedly fighting to liberate a country was a heady thing and Jeff still found himself occasionally caught up in the rhetoric. Easy, that is, until they arrived at their next temporary base one day in late April—a large *hacienda* that the *Villaistas* would be occupying for a while according to one of the men.

The *hacienda* was big by anyone's standards. It was owned by an American who had taken up residence some years prior after he had married a local girl. He later had become a citizen of Mexico.

The owner, Marc Richardson, was a mild-mannered liberal sort of fellow who had always provided aid and comfort to any of the rebels in the area who happened by his *hacienda*.

When Pancho Villa showed up with his

army, the rancher was completely taken aback. Providing a meal and a straw bed in the livery stable for a small number of men was one thing, but supplying food and water for as many as a hundred men as well as their horses would put a marked strain on his ranch, especially during a drought year.

After being told to get ready to take some photographs, Jeff Shaw began going through his equipment in the yard in front of the main house. The setting provided a panoramic view of the surrounding area, which pleased Jeff.

Usually, Marc Richardson was somewhat timid, but first and foremost he was a businessman. He couldn't help but protest such a large intrusion onto his ranch. Both he and his wife, a middle-aged but still very attractive woman, approached the rebel general on foot.

Watching his men as they dismounted, Villa remained in the saddle on his favorite bay horse. Behind him stood Mercedes and several of his more trusted officers, including Julio Cardenas. The rest of Villa's army was fanned out around the yard, many still mounted.

While he was fluent in Spanish, in times of stress Marc Richardson reverted to his native English. "You are welcome to our ranch, General, to water your horses, rest a bit, but then you must be on your way. We simply are not equipped to handle this many . . . men. We are sorry."

As soon as the man had begun speaking in English, Mercedes started translating for Villa.

"I'm sure you understand, General," Richardson concluded, shrugging. His wife remained at his side, nodding, as he explained the situation, but glancing nervously at the band of soldiers closing in on them. She began to tremble.

"Understand?" Villa suddenly roared in Spanish. "I understand very well. You do not support the revolution. You are just like all the other *hacendados*."

That last word in Spanish meant land baron, and had become a smear that was practically synonymous with the very reason for the revolution. The negative aspect to the word *hacendado* implied, however falsely, that any large ranch owner must be guilty of corruption, and must have gained his wealth off the backs of hardworking innocent *peones*. The fact that such ranches produced herds of cattle or large crops and gave jobs to many who would otherwise starve was irrelevant. To the uneducated masses, they were robber barons.

Jeff, who had remained in the buckboard, was struck by the general's sudden eruption of temper and total change of personality. Shaw was suddenly very scared for the first time in many days.

"¡*Gringo pendejo*!" Villa cursed. "You come to

our country, steal our land, take our women, and rob our people."

Richardson threw his hands up in protest. "*Mi general*, you know that is not true." He began backing up with his hands raised as Villa deliberately drew his pistol. Then he fired four shots into the unarmed rancher's chest.

Richardson slumped to the ground as his terrified wife screamed.

"You killed him, you coward! You are a murdering pig!" she yelled back at Villa.

The general looked down at her and turned to some of his men who were standing nearby. "Take this whore away and teach her what we think of those of our women who prostitute themselves to foreigners."

Several of the rebels looked at the woman and grinned cravenly. They looked to Villa for a final confirmation.

Villa nodded. "You understood me perfectly. Now get her out of my sight. Do what you want with her. ¡*Andale, muchachos*!"

Seven of the men rushed the terrified woman and dragged her into the main house as she kicked and pleaded.

Her screams could be heard from the second floor for the better part of an hour.

Jeff watched as the men came out of the house, laughing. He wished he had never seen or heard of Mr. and Mrs. Richardson.

Mercedes didn't know what to say or do. She was stunned. She had seen her general angry and on occasion behave fiercely in battle, but she had never known this side of him. It was right then and there that Mercedes made up her mind that she no longer wished to be associated with such a cold-blooded villain. However, she knew that she could not simply resign and leave. She feared that to even have such thoughts could lead to a fate similar to that of *Señora* Richardson.

Later that afternoon General Villa ordered his men to line up in the front yard near a rustic well so that Jeff could document the heroic battle to liberate this *hacienda* in the name of Villa's homeland.

Reluctantly, Jeff did as requested, but when the time came for him to sight his camera on Pancho Villa and his group, he wished to God that instead of pushing the flash button on the camera he was pulling the trigger of a rifle.

Chapter Eighteen

Since their encounter with the gang of *bandidos* in the cañon, Thad McCallum and Pedro Peralta had been riding due south for over three weeks. They had seen little except miles and miles of more miles and miles. It was hot and dusty and both men were in a rough mood.

That evening the two men made camp in a small grove of trees. They loosely hobbled the horses and mules in a particularly lush area so the stock could graze as much as they wanted without wandering off.

Later, after a dinner of beans, boiled rice, tortillas, and some canned peaches, the two sat and enjoyed a cup of trail-brewed coffee.

"Guess the older I get the more impatient I become," McCallum commented out loud as he lit his pipe. It was directed as much to himself as to his friend.

"How so, *jefe*?" Pedro inquired.

"Well, for one thing, back when I was working for the Pinkertons, I could go on the trail of someone for months and not give a second thought about what day it was or how soon I had to get back."

"True, *jefe*, but you weren't tied down back

then. Now you have a ranch and your crew to worry about."

McCallum thought it over and nodded. "Maybe you're right, but, even so, it's been weeks and there's still no sight of Villa's army or the boy. Surely by now we'd have seen or heard something. Anything."

Pedro shook his head. "No, *jefe*, not necessarily. It is a big country and Villa, he is constantly on the move. Remember, the Mexican government is looking for him, too. He knows if he stands still, the *federales*, they will find him. Plus, the *gringo* army is also in this now. Pancho Villa may be many things, but he is no fool. If he knows the American military has moved into Mexico, he knows they are after him and that they won't stop until they get him."

Thad agreed. "Yeah, you can say that again. Black Jack Pershing ain't got no back-up in him whatsoever."

"Neither do you, *jefe*, neither do you. So, stop worrying. We will find this boy, one way or another."

"Yeah, but it's the one way or another that I'm worried about, Pedro," McCallum replied.

"Surely when you were a detective you must have felt like this many times, I'm thinking." After all these years, Pedro knew most of his friend's stories by heart, but he was trying to draw McCallum into a conversation that would take his mind off their worries. "Didn't you ever have a case that took longer to finish than you expected? A man you couldn't catch?" Pedro asked before taking a sip his coffee.

McCallum chuckled, remembering the old days. "Of course. Sure there was. In fact, I once went after this one particular con man who kept changing identities on me so often it felt like I was chasing a ghost."

"That so? Clever fellow he was?" Pedro asked, smiling to himself.

Thad poured himself another cup of coffee, set his pipe down for a moment, and popped a piece of licorice in his mouth. "Clever would be putting it mildly," he replied, pressing a hand to his stomach to ease the discomfort of his attack of indigestion.

"His name was Gary Simmons, if I remember correctly, but he went by a dozen or more aliases. He worked his cons all over the country. I got involved after he left Chicago to go West and the Pinks got called in."

"So why did they send you after him?" Pedro asked.

"Well, he kept on the move so often, he'd be out of the local law's jurisdiction before you could say Davy Crockett. Sheriffs had put out warrant after warrant on him, but this Simmons was a smart one. He'd change his looks . . . grow a beard, or wear an eye patch . . . just to confuse anyone who paid attention to the Wanted posters."

"And so?" Pedro said, encouraging his friend.

"Well, let's see. One of his con jobs turned out to be an embezzlement scheme he pulled on a rich Chicago railroad baron who had no forgiveness in his soul. Man by the name of Aaron Phillips. He got so fed up waiting on the law, he hired the Pinkertons to track this Simmons fellow down."

Thad put his coffee cup aside, picked up his pipe, and re-lit it. "As I remember, Mister Phillips said he would double the posted reward, but only on the condition that we bring Simmons back to Chicago and drop him off at Phillips's office and leave the two of them alone for a half hour before taking him to the police station."

"I can imagine what he had in mind for that little reunion," Pedro chuckled. "Phillips being a railroad man and all, no, *jefe*?"

McCallum nodded, grinning. "Yeah, but better you don't ask about that part. At any rate when the Pinks found out that Simmons had left Illinois, heading for the western plains, they notified my office and I took the assignment. At first I thought it was going to be rather routine, but, like I said, this Gary Simmons fellow was trickier than a Mississippi cardsharp."

"How so?" Pedro asked.

"Seems like he carried at least five full changes

of clothes wherever he went and constantly traded horses. He made sure there was nothing to distinguish him from the crowd. He had no characteristic habits, never worked with a partner, and there was never anyone other than his victims who knew him well enough to identify him."

"So, how'd you find him?" Pedro asked.

Thad blew a cloud of smoke and thought for a moment. "Well, over the years I'd noticed that men on the run usually use aliases that are similar to their own names. It makes it easier for them to remember who they are supposed to be. Robert Smith might change to Richard Schmidt or Jake Thompson might be changed to Jack Thomas. Get the idea?" Pedro nodded over his cup of coffee. "So, I went to the towns where his scams had been run and started collecting names."

"That doesn't seem like it would be of much help if he already had left town," Pedro observed.

"That alone wouldn't be, but next I began marking all his previously known locations on a map. After a while I noticed a pattern."

"A pattern, *jefe*?"

"Sure. You see, most criminals always make some small mistake that turns out to be their Achilles' heel. I noticed that Gary Simmons always traveled from big city to big city. After all, that's where the money is, not in small backwater hick towns."

"That's true enough, I think," Pedro observed, rolling up a cigarette.

Thad continued his tale. "His flaw was that, instead of traveling from city to city in a random fashion, north, south, east, or west, he seemed to me to be traveling toward San Francisco in an upside-down curve on my map. Then I noticed he was usually last seen in banks and telegraph offices. It stood to reason he was wiring his ill-gotten money ahead in case he was caught and searched, or even robbed on the trail. Fact is, criminals ride on stagecoaches and railroads just like normal folks do, and, as we well know, these occasionally get robbed."

"So, *jefe*, if he was so tricky what did you do to finally catch him?" Pedro asked lighting his cigarette.

McCallum smiled broadly and fiddled a moment with his pipe, rubbing the bowl wood with his thumb. "I traced out the next two big cities on the curve of my map, and then, using this hunch, I traveled to the second city as fast as I could, skipping the city I believed was his next destination. Since Simmons often used name variations of the abbreviations GS and because I figured that, sooner or later, once he arrived, he would want to pick up the money he had wired, I staked out the telegrapher's office."

"Very clever move," Pedro agreed.

"Turned out that way," McCallum replied. "A few well-placed bills helped convince the station operator to tip me off when a Gregg or Gary or Gavin with a last name starting with the letter S arrived to pick up a money transfer. The rest, as they say, was history. I turned him over to another agent for transport the rest of the way back to the Windy City."

Peralta looked perplexed.

"It's what they call Chicago, Illinois," McCallum explained.

Pedro nodded. "*Bravo, jefe.* Very well done."

Thad tapped the tobacco ashes from his pipe. "Yep. That's what that fellow Phillips from Chicago said when our agent showed up at his office with Simmons in cuffs. Word is Simmons ended up at the police station alive, but not much else."

Chapter Nineteen

H e's gone completely off his rocker," Jeff said quietly to Mercedes. They were standing in a dark corner behind the *hacienda*'s stables. "I can't continue with this. I've got to get away."

"You will die trying," Mercedes replied. She hesitated before adding: "I don't want any harm to come to you, *mi querido*."

"My love?" Jeff repeated, realizing what she had just said. "So, you do care for me as much as I do for you."

"Julio would kill us both if he were to find out," Mercedes remarked sadly. She was obviously worried and afraid.

"I don't care. I'd rather die than think of you ending up with him for good," Jeff said angrily.

Mercedes glanced around the corner, making sure that no one could hear or see them. "Then we must plan our escape very carefully. We will need horses, food, and water. Can you shoot a gun?" she asked.

"I may not be the strongest or smartest man you ever met, but I am the son of a soldier," Jeff replied proudly. "If it fires, I can shoot it, and I usually hit whatever I aim at. Hell, I was taught to shoot before I learned the alphabet. That's one thing my father taught me."

Mercedes's expression was clearly one of doubt.

Jeff frowned. "Fine, don't believe me. Obviously, I can't play William Tell here, so you will just have to trust me."

Puzzled, Mercedes asked: "Who is this William person?"

"An old Army marksman," Jeff joked. "He taught my father." She looked at him curiously. "Don't worry, I can handle myself if given half a chance."

"Julio won't give you half a chance, and now I believe Villa won't give you even that much if he catches you escaping." She considered things for a moment, and then added: "Maybe if I were to help you get away first, I could join you later."

Jeff shook his head. "You got me all wrong, sweetheart. I'm not the sort to leave here without you," he insisted. He took her in his arms and kissed her, long and hard. She melted into his embrace. Jeff was a little surprised at his new-found confidence around Mercedes.

After a few brief moments of tenderness, Mercedes pulled away, straightened her hair, and looked up at the face of the one whom she now realized was, as old-fashioned as it sounds, her one true love.

"We shall see, *mi querdio*, we shall see. But for now, I need to think and plan," she said firmly.

"Mercedes! *¿Donde estás?*" a voice suddenly yelled out from the darkness.

"It's Julio," Mercedes cried, recognizing his voice. "He's looking for me. You must go, Jeff. He must not catch us together. Please, go. Hurry!"

Shaw shook his head. "Give me a gun and I'll kill that son-of-a-bitch right here and now!"

Mercedes was shocked at the intensity of his outburst. "Don't be a fool. Even if you did manage to kill him, every gun in the camp would finish you off, and *pronto*. Now go, that way . . . around the back of the barn." She gave him a quick kiss on the lips.

"The thought of you being with him is unbearable," Jeff replied.

Mercedes smiled at him and made a get-going gesture with her hands. "Better unbearable than dead. Now go!"

Jeff shrugged and hurried away into the night. Behind him, he heard Mercedes shout out: "*¡Aqui, Julio, here I am!*" Jeff shuddered with anger and jealousy.

"What are you doing here at this hour?" Julio asked. He was clearly suspicious.

"I was checking on my horse. I was worried . . . he's been off his feed lately. I thought it might be colic," Mercedes replied.

"Colic, huh? So, how is he?"

Mercedes answered without hesitation. "He

seems to be eating better tonight, but not as much as he usually eats."

Julio nodded. *"Bueno.* So, where is the *gringo?"*

"How should I know?" she hissed scornfully. "At this time of night, he's probably sleeping in his tent or over at his wagon. Why do you ask me?"

"Just you stay away from him," Cardenas ordered. "You hear me? You are my woman."

Mercedes glared at him with fire in her eyes. "Understand this, Julio. I am not anyone's woman. I am a *Villaista.* I will be with whomever I choose, whether you like it or not." Then to calm down the captain she pressed her hands on his chest. *"Cálmate, chico.* Relax. Think about it. Why in the world would I choose such a boy over a man like you? And a *gringo* besides?"

Cardenas looked at Mercedes lustily. "So then come back to the big house with me," he replied encouragingly.

"I would, Julio, but I am going to stay with my horse for a while, and then I am going to take a bath and go to sleep. You wouldn't want me smelling like a horse now, would you?"

Cardenas smiled wickedly. "Oh, wouldn't I?"

"Cerdo." She laughed. "You might want to consider taking a bath, too. Now leave me be and go." Mercedes gave him a small kiss on the cheek and pushed him away.

169

Julio Cardenas grunted and walked off. Mercedes suddenly went weak in the knees and had to lean against the stable wall for support. She knew it was a very dangerous game she was playing. She shook her head and mumbled aloud: "*Ay, chica*, what have you gotten yourself into now?"

Chapter Twenty

Following the Columbus raid the usual and expected political negotiations took place between the United States and Mexico. While the Army started making its preparations for the punitive expedition, United States Secretary of State Lansing began to negotiate with Mexico's President Venustiano Carranza to allow the United States to enter Mexico without his government's interference.

At first *El Presidente* balked at granting approval for such an invasive expedition into his country. Carranza had insisted that his own troops could track down Villa. The United States, however, flatly refused this offer, and after a week of back and forth negotiations, Carranza's government reluctantly agreed to allow the Americans to cross the border with the condition that they went no farther than the state of Chihuahua.

When General John J. Pershing finally crossed the Río Grande, he did so at the head of an enormous Army. He had a long line of horses, mules, and some primitive Dodge cars and trucks. The trucks were valuable because the Mexicans had initially refused access to their railways.

To complicate things further, local authorities

continuously cut the telegraph lines that the Army had laid.

Eventually President Carranza agreed to limited use of Mexico's railways, but by that time the Army had already set up its own supply routes to follow Pershing into Chihuahua.

By April 8th, the American expedition was more than four hundred miles into Mexico with a total troop strength of almost seven thousand men. The force was divided into two flying columns with orders to search for Pancho Villa, who was believed to be making his main base camp at Casas Grandes, Chihuahua.

Because of the continued disputes with the Carranza administration over the use of the Mexican North Western railway to supply Pershing's troops, the United States Army employed trucks for the first time to convoy supplies to Pershing's headquarters. The expedition set up its headquarters in the town of Colonia Dublan. Its supply base was located on a large tract of land near the Casas Grandes River.

Since he had no idea how long he would be in Chihuahua or how much farther south he would have to penetrate before locating Villa, General Pershing wanted to ensure that his Army was well supplied.

When the expedition had been denied the full use of the Mexican railway system, Pershing turned to his motor transport companies to pick up the slack. The problem with that was that the Army did not have nearly enough trucks to transport all the needed food, clothing, weapons, and ammunition that had been stored in Columbus.

Pershing's Punitive Expedition, as it came to be known, started out as a logistical nightmare. Nothing of this magnitude had ever been attempted by the U.S. Army on foreign soil. Word of this dilemma was eventually forwarded back to the Secretary of War Newton Baker, who somehow managed to appropriate $450,000 in government funds to purchase new trucks.

The government's money was well spent as eventually more than ten thousand tons of supplies were delivered to Pershing's army by these vehicles. Moving supplies by truck, never an easy feat, was made worse during this expedition because the routes depicted on available maps turned out to be nothing more than rough trails that were hopelessly impassable during inclement weather.

As a result, Army engineers were forced to rebuild many of the Mexican roads. To a large extent, the expedition still had to rely on mules and wagons to keep its supplies moving.

General Pershing picked a young West Point second lieutenant from the 8th Cavalry, George S. Patton, Jr., as his aide-de-camp. As such Lieutenant Patton was tasked with overseeing the logistics of Pershing's transportation as well as acting as the general's personal courier.

In mid-April, Second Lieutenant Patton, always the eager military fire-eater, asked General Pershing for the opportunity to command troops of his own, and so was re-attached to the 13th Cavalry to assist in the manhunt for Pancho Villa and his subordinates.

Chapter Twenty-One

McCallum looked over his map. "How far is it to the next town?" he asked Pedro. The two men had stopped by a small creek to water and rest their horses. It had been a solid week of hard riding across a barren landscape.

Pedro pushed his sombrero up higher on his head and, putting his hand over his eyes to block the glare of the sun, stared off into the distance. "I would say two more days' ride and we should be there, *jefe*. Maybe less."

McCallum popped some licorice into his mouth and sighed. "I sure could use a fresh bath and a nice cold beer."

His friend nodded in agreement. "A pretty *señorita* playing a *guitarra* wouldn't be so bad, either."

Thad laughed and nodded his head. "Wouldn't be half bad at that, but, knowing you, it would probably take a couple of horses and mules to pull you away. Wouldn't mind it myself iffen it wasn't for that damned boy down here."

"Don't worry, *jefe*, we'll find him," Peralta assured McCallum.

"Well, I'll tell you what, Pedro. We find that boy in one piece, I'll find you that *señorita*. How's that sound?"

Pedro chuckled and picked up his reins. "*Sí, jefe*, you have a deal."

When they finally rode into town, it was a toss-up as to which was more run down, Thad, Pedro, or the livestock. McCallum was beginning to think that they were destined to ride forever, visiting small Mexican towns that were all mirror images of each other. He was tired and annoyed at their lack of progress. His body ached for a nice thick bed with a thick pillow or two.

Even as exhausted as they were from their ride, the two rode to the livery stable first. After all, no true rider cares for himself before his horse.

Once dismounted, McCallum clung to his saddle for a moment before leading his horse inside.

"You all right, *jefe*?" Pedro asked, concerned.

McCallum took a deep breath and sighed. "Knees locked up on me for a moment. I'm all right. Just got to get the blood circulating." He shook his legs a mite and arched his back. "I'm fine. Let's get these animals boarded, and then see about a room and a bath. If it's all right with you, let's worry about *señoritas* some other time. Damn, I hate this growing old horse-shit."

"Fine with me, *jefe*, whatever you say."

They found a suitable hotel about five blocks

from the livery stable. The sign read Hotel La Sombra, or loosely translated, the Shady Inn. McCallum hoped it would provide some cool comfortable shade for a change.

Pedro arranged for two rooms on the second floor with the hotel's desk clerk, a short, rotund fellow with a droopy black mustache. Although he appeared unfazed about having an *Americano* in his hotel, Pedro noticed the man's eyes never left McCallum's back.

"Which one do you want, Pedro?" McCallum asked, opening the door to the first room.

"They are probably alike, so you go ahead and take this one," Pedro replied. "I'll take the one across the hall, here."

"Meet you for dinner at seven tonight," McCallum stated. "I'm gonna take a bath, if there's one available, and then doze off till my stomach wakes me."

"Sounds good to me, *jefe. Hasta luego*," Pedro replied.

McCallum examined the room for a moment. He always read any new room he entered. It was an old habit, usually unnecessary, but on occa-sion it had saved him from the occasional surprise, especially back in the Pinkerton days.

It was a typical hotel room. Along the left side of the room was a single four-poster bed with a white and red quilt on it. Above the bed on the wall was a rather crudely painted mural depicting a waterfall with what Thad assumed was a deer in the background. Either that or it was a funny-looking dog with antlers.

To the right of the bed was a cabinet with a ceramic basin and a large mirror above it that rotated front to back. There was also a small, rose-patterned towel hanging on a small rod off to the side of the cabinet.

On the other side of the room was a decent-sized wardrobe. McCallum stood to one side as he opened the door. One time, back in St. Louis, there had been a surprise guest hiding inside a similar wardrobe, intent on separating McCallum from any cash he might have on hand.

The result had been a poor one for the would-be thief who was promptly taught how to do an acrobatic circus-like act right out the hotel window. Sadly, in that incident, there had been no safety net on the ground beneath Thad's fourth-floor room.

Fortunately, this time the room and its closet, while showing age, held no surprises. McCallum hung his hat and holster on a rack near the door, removed his boots, and flopped on the bed. He was asleep as soon as his head hit the pillow.

Chapter Twenty-Two

A map was spread out on the long wooden table that had been set up in a tent. Bent over the map was General John J. Pershing. Standing next to him in the tent were his aide-de-camp and two civilian guides.

"Are you sure about this information?" Pershing asked.

"As sure as you can be in this country," the taller of the two guides answered. His name was E. L. Holmdahl. "To date, the contacts we share have been accurate, but one never knows. Honestly, General, some of those we work with may be closet *Villaistas*. Remember, Villa has been on the run from his own government for years without getting caught. He's like a damned Robin Hood," Holmdahl explained.

"Well, I'm sure as hell not the Sheriff of Nottingham," Pershing replied angrily. "I would have burned the whole of Sherwood Forest right down to the ground." The general pointed to a spot on his map. "This ranch here . . . has anyone checked it out yet?" he asked.

The other men in the tent glanced over the general's shoulder. They all shook their heads. "No, sir, not yet."

"Well, maybe Villa is there right now, or

perhaps he's visited it recently. Maybe his army is headed that way," Pershing opined. "Regardless, we need to send a patrol to check out this ranch. Understood?"

"Yes, sir. Will do," Pershing's aide replied smartly.

The general thought for a moment before he said: "Let Georgie Patton lead it. We need a young lion for this one and he's been itching to get into combat." Then as an afterthought, he added: "And have him take these two guides along with him. If you have no objections?"

The two men shook their heads, indicating they were willing to help.

"Tell him to take those Dodge cars. Might do him good to get off a horse for once."

The aide laughed while the two civilians nodded. It was well known among the head-quarters staff that Patton came from a very wealthy family and had practically grown up riding polo ponies and dressage horses. George Patton was a cavalryman to the core and a personal favorite of Pershing's because of his enthusiasm and raw determination.

After writing out the general's instructions, the aide placed them in an envelope and sealed them. He then turned and saluted, lifted the tent flap, and disappeared into the Army's camp.

At the time Second Lieutenant George S. Patton was to receive his new orders he was in Troop C of the 13th Cavalry. When Pershing's aide found him, Patton was standing outside his tent, practicing with a model 1913 cavalry saber. This model of sword would later become known as the Patton sword, because of his input in designing it while he was assigned to Fort Meyers.

Patton had been an Olympic-level fencer, having finished fourth in the 1912 Olympic Games in Stockholm, Sweden. He also finished sixth in the equestrian events, and would have won the pistol competition had it not been for a controversy regarding his shot placement. While most competitors in the games used .22-caliber pistols, Patton chose to compete with a .38 revolver. He claimed that due to the size of the holes it produced, some of his bullets went through the same hole.

Although such a level of accuracy is possible, and although a total miss was highly unlikely with Patton's level of proficiency, there was no way to prove it. The judges at the time ruled that his shots had missed the target and subsequently he lost the event. The soldier took the loss as a sportsman and as a gentleman, and was well respected for his conduct by his competitors.

"Lieutenant Patton, I have orders for you," Pershing's aide announced, handing him an envelope. "Right from the general."

"Finally," Patton replied, tossing the sword onto the cot inside his tent. "Hopefully it's some action. It's already May and all I've been allowed to shoot at was a damned rattlesnake and a couple of mangy coyotes."

The aide smiled back at him. "Open it and see for yourself, Georgie."

Patton took a moment or two to review the orders and nodded. "Great. But just where the hell is this San Miguelito Ranch?" he asked.

"Supposed to be somewhere near Rubio, Chihuahua," the aide replied. "Guess you'll have to find a map. Also, General Pershing has a couple of civilian guides he wants to go along with you. Mister Holmdahl and a friend of his. I believe they know where this place is."

"We sure Villa's men are there?" Patton asked.

The aide shook his head. "Nope. Haven't got a clue. This one's by guess and by golly. We just don't know for sure, but I can tell you that the reports I've seen indicate it's likely there will be some sort of action. Truthfully, I just don't know what kind, if any, or how much, or how bad it will be."

The young lieutenant re-read the orders, folded the papers, and put them in his breast pocket, smiling. "I'll need a couple of hours to pick the men and horses. We'll probably need some pack mules, too. You riding with us?"

The officer shook his head. "Sadly, not this time. It's all your show. Oh, and, Georgie, you won't be riding any horses this time."

Patton looked both surprised and disappointed. Any visions of a glorious cavalry charge had suddenly faded away. "Then how the hell are we supposed to get there? Swim?" he asked.

"Well, you'll be riding all right, but the general wants you to take your men out in those three new Dodge touring cars. Wants to see how well they hold up on patrol," the aide explained.

Patton groaned. "Cars? What is this . . . the cavalry or the New York taxi cab service?"

Pershing's aide shrugged. "Got to think modern, Lieutenant Patton. You get to be the first one to replace saddle sores with tire marks. Now take ten men and those two guides and find us some Mexican rebels."

"If they are out there, I'll find the bastards. You can count on it. If the god-damned cars don't get a flat or run out of gas, that is!" Patton replied angrily.

The officer laughed. Patton was already creating quite a reputation for his rather colorful language. "I always did appreciate your confidence, Lieutenant. Just don't forget to take some extra gas and a spare tire or two. I think those cars have a rather big trunk, don't they?" He flipped Patton a friendly and casual salute.

Patton returned the salute in like manner, and joked: "Maybe I'll get a chance to notch this pistol of mine, after all."

For a time, Patton had carried a model M1911

Colt semi-automatic pistol until it accidentally discharged through his belt. Since then he had replaced it with a Colt .45 single-action revolver.

Unlike his fellow officers, George Patton came from a very affluent family. He had bought a custom upgraded silver-plated version and had its wooden grips replaced with ivory ones.

Patton had originally asked the man who sold him the pistol about having pearl handles put on it. But the salesman insisted that, although they were slightly more expensive, ivory grips were preferable.

"Ivory provides the shooter's hand a better gripping surface with less slippage," the salesman had said. "Besides," he added, "only a pimp from a cheap Louisiana whorehouse wears pearl handles."

Patton loved that line so much that he made it his trademark response whenever anyone asked him about his fancy pistol.

The aide turned to leave. "Good luck, Georgie. And remember to bring me back one of those big round sombreros."

Lieutenant George Patton was never one to avoid self-promotion whenever possible. "Hell, I'll bring you back the fellow wearing it and dump the body at the general's tent flap. You can pick it off him yourself," he bragged.

The aide just shook his head in amusement before returning to his duties.

Chapter Twenty-Three

Thad McCallum was ready to meet Pedro for dinner. He briefly considered leaving his Winchester rifle in the corner of his hotel room but decided against it. There were two reasons. First, he didn't completely trust hotel rooms and didn't want his favorite rifle stolen. More importantly, he reasoned that a firearm is only good when you have it available to use.

Although the hotel was pleasant enough, he was in a foreign country with people unknown to him all around. He picked up his rifle and, tucking it under his arm, locked the door and went down the stairs to the main lobby.

Pedro was waiting for him in the hotel bar. No matter the situation, it always seemed Thad's friend was ready before he was. Pedro motioned for McCallum to join him. "Have a beer, *jefe*?"

McCallum nodded and Pedro said something to the barman who leaned under the bar and brought out a bottle of beer. Thad held it up to the light. "What, no worm in it?"

Peralta shook his head. "They only put the worm in mescal. You know that, *jefe*."

"Worm's too good to waste on just plain beer, I guess," Thad joked.

"*Salud*," Pedro said, raising his bottle in the typical Mexican toast.

"To your good health, my friend," Thad replied, clinking his bottle against Pedro's. "Now let's get something to eat, and then go find this lad before I die of old age."

"Well, then, we better hurry, I think," Peralta said.

"Oh, screw you and the horse you rode in on. You're almost as old as I am," Thad remarked.

"My point exactly," Pedro said.

Thad finished his beer and the two men went to the dining area and chose a table against the far wall.

Pedro ordered tortilla soup and a plate of cheese enchiladas with refried beans. McCallum decided to stick with steak and potatoes. While the food was being served, Thad noticed one of the waiters leaning on a table at the far end of the room. The man had a dark complexion like most do south of the border, but his features were different. When he walked past their table later, McCallum caught the man's arm. The waiter didn't seem startled and simply turned to face him. The man's face was expressionless, but his body was clearly tensed.

"Chiricahua or Mescalero?" McCallum asked quietly.

The waiter looked at him as if sizing up an opponent. After a moment's hesitation, he replied: "Both."

"How so?" McCallum asked in the Apache language.

The man relaxed. He was obviously surprised. "You speak our language?" It was more a question than a statement of the obvious.

McCallum nodded back at the man. "How so?" McCallum asked again.

"Father was Chiricahua, and mother was of the Mescalero band," he explained.

"My name is Thaddeus McCallum and this is Pedro Peralta, my blood brother."

"My name is Skinyea," the Apache replied. McCallum had noticed over the years that some Indians were reluctant to refer to themselves directly, but not this one.

"Means cañon, doesn't it?" McCallum asked.

The man nodded. "How you speak Apache?"

"You speak English," Thad observed, and then continued in English himself. "When I was younger my Army troop was assigned to your tribe's area. I also became friends with a white man named Thomas Jeffords. You know this name? Tom Jeffords?"

The Indian nodded. Jeffords was well known throughout the Southwest by whites and Indian tribes alike. In the late 1860s Jeffords was the superintendent of an independent mail line that was about to be incorporated into the Pony Express.

After several of his mail riders were killed by Apaches, Jeffords decided that something had to be done to end the bloodshed. He proceeded to learn enough of the Apache language to get by, and then saddled up and rode alone into Cochise's camp.

It is said that when Jeffords finally came face-to-face with the head of those fearsome Chiricahuas, he unbuckled his gun belt and holster and handed them to Cochise. As the story goes, he requested that the Chiricahua leader have one of the women hold them for him while Jeffords was in their camp and that he could retrieve them when he was ready to leave. The implication of course was that he expected to be allowed to leave.

They say that Cochise was so impressed with the man's courage that he granted Jeffords safe passage though Apache lands. Their friendship later lead to the famous meeting of Cochise with General Oliver Howard in 1871 and the subsequent peace treaty of 1872.

To his dying day, General Howard always credited Jeffords with being the one who was primarily responsible for bringing peace to the region. Jeffords was later appointed Indian agent for the Chiricahua Mountain area.

A truly remarkable man, Tom Jeffords was

later a stagecoach driver, a deputy sheriff for Tombstone, Arizona, and a gold prospector. He lived out his last twenty-two years in the Tortolita Mountains north of Tucson, Arizona, dying in 1914.

The waiter nodded back at McCallum. "I was friend of Cochise."

"And I was friend of Jeffords," Thad said, before continuing. "My friend, Pedro, and I are seeking a friend who was taken by a band of outlaw Mexicans. It is said they are many and powerful. The outlaws are led by a man called Villa. Pancho Villa." McCallum spoke quietly since he had no way of knowing the sentiments of the hotel patrons. "You know this man?" he asked.

The Apache's eyes were expressionless as usual. After a moment or two he grunted. "Villa, *sí*. This man is well known by many men."

"The reason we are trying to find this young man who was kidnapped is that his mother is sick and would like us to find him. We do not know where he is or who we can trust. Could you help us?"

Pedro added: "We will gladly pay you for your troubles."

The Apache looked around the room before speaking. The room was not crowded and no one seemed interested in them. "I will ask what you seek among my people. Meet me behind the hotel in the place where it is dark between the buildings. I will be there when the sun goes down."

The Apache Skinyea then picked up the empty plates from the table and headed toward the hotel kitchen.

After they finished their after-dinner coffee, the two men rose to leave the room when Pedro was bumped by a large man. As far as McCallum could see, there had been plenty of room to get by. He concluded the shove must have been intentional.

Even under duress Pedro Peralta was a relatively calm individual and never purposely sought out confrontation, so it was only natural that, whether it was his fault or not, he would be the one to apologize.

"*Perdón, señor*," Pedro said.

The man looked down at Pedro with disgust. "You dress like a *vaquero*, but you eat with *gringos* and kiss ass with Apaches. Go screw yourself, *cabrón*."

In this situation, Thad tensed at the word *gringo*. It is an oft used Mexican slur that is believed to date back to the Mexican-American War when the invading American soldiers all wore green uniforms. The sound of "green goes" eventually became part of the Mexican lingo. Thus, *gringos*.

While it may have been a common word, it

is often not what is said that is significant, but rather how it is said. Besides, Thad knew that the Spanish word *cabrón* was a much worse slur. He also knew that south of the border even a person as mellow as Pedro would never tolerate a stranger calling him a bastard.

Instinctively, McCallum undid the thong from his pistol's hammer and looked around, trying to determine if the large man was alone. He was twice Peralta's size, but McCallum wasn't overly concerned. He knew his friend's abilities. Pedro knew two things extremely well: taming horses and doing the same with people.

"Stranger," Peralta said in Spanish, "were you speaking to me? I'm sorry, but I didn't quite understand what you were saying. You see, I do not know how to speak stupidly like you do."

Deep down Thad groaned. There would be no avoiding a confrontation now.

The big Mexican filled with rage and was about to attack when he felt a pistol barrel up against his back.

"Not here, *muchacho*, outside," Thad said quietly.

"When I'm done with this cockroach, you'll be next," the man growled at Pedro.

"I doubt it very much, but we'll see," Pedro replied. "Now, outside. We wouldn't want to make a scene in such a nice dining room."

The large man walked slowly through the door.

McCallum kept the pressure on the man's back with his pistol until they were well out into the street.

"Very brave of you, *gringo*, especially when I have no gun," the man growled.

"Pedro?" Thad said. His friend was removing his gun belt.

"Don't worry about the *Americano*," Pedro said to the big man. "All you have to worry about is this little cockroach." He then handed his gun rig to Thad.

A crowd was beginning to form, made up of a few people from inside the hotel and some passers-by from the street. McCallum watched for any sign of a weapon being drawn among those in the group, but seemed satisfied that, at least for now, this would be a contest of strength or, in his friend's case, ability.

"Any particular rules?" Pedro asked.

"*Chinga tu madre*," the man replied, uttering one of Mexico's worst curses.

"Not likely," Pedro replied quietly. "All right, then. No rules it is."

The man rushed Peralta and grabbed him in a front bear hug.

Given his size, Thad considered intervening for a moment. Pedro saw him out of the corner of his eye, and shook his head, so McCallum reluctantly holstered his Colt.

The man had wrapped his big arms inside

Pedro's arms and around his chest. He was completely capable of crushing Pedro's ribs, but in his rush, he had left Peralta's arms free.

There is a soft notch under the front of a person's throat that leads downward into the thorax. Regardless of a man's muscular strength there is almost no way to toughen this spot against a blow, a fact about which Pedro was aware.

Even though the wind was being crushed out of him, it took almost no effort for Pedro to shove the tips of his fingers in and down into that throat notch.

The other man choked, released his grip, and stumbled backward. Pedro arched his back slightly to relieve the pain before squaring off to face his opponent.

The man spit and again rushed the small *vaquero*. This time Pedro waited till the last moment, then simply side-stepped while kicking straight forward with the inside of his boot. It was the same type of kick children in Mexico use to play their form of *fútbol* that Americans call soccer.

Peralta's boot connected with the big man's shin so hard he went face down into the dirt. The sound of the kick connecting was so loud that for a second McCallum wondered if the man's shin had been broken.

To his credit the big Mexican was no quitter

and tried quickly to get up. Even though he gained his feet, he hobbled as he moved toward Pedro.

"*¿Suficiente, amigo?*" Pedro asked, giving his opponent an out.

Instead of replying, the man suddenly lunged, grabbing Pedro by the front of his vest in an attempt to head-butt him.

However, Peralta knew what was coming and, after clamping his arms over the other man's grip, turned his upper torso sideways to avoid the blow. The twisting motion threw the big man off balance to his left, and as he tried to regain his stance, Pedro loosened his arms and quickly grabbed the man's thumbs, prying them off his vest.

Actually, he did more than pry. He bent the thumbs of his adversary backward until they both snapped. As the man bent forward in agony, Pedro raised his knee up and struck the man squarely in the face. The big Mexican passed out in the street.

Peralta walked back to his friend and retrieved his holster. He had hardly even worked up a sweat.

In all their time together, McCallum had never found out exactly where his friend had learned to fight so adeptly. McCallum had been taught by many good Army self-defense instructors, but the training was mostly straight boxing and wrestling. He had seen several demonstrations of Indian wrestling tactics and once saw a display given by a visiting Japanese officer of something called *jujitsu*. Pedro's fighting abilities in combat were similar to those styles, but as often as Thad had tried to find out more about his friend's past instruction, all he could get out of him was that he had learned how to fight from his grand-father. McCallum always thought that Pedro's grandfather must have been one hell of a man.

Pedro turned to the crowd and told them to go home. Then, pointing to his friend, he said loud enough for all to hear: "*Este Americano es mi amigo y es un buen hombre.*" The implication was clear—mess with him and you mess with me. The crowd immediately dispersed.

Once it was dark, McCallum and Peralta went to meet the Apache. Thad did not like dark alleys, nor did Pedro. Before heading to the back of the hotel, both men checked the cylinders of their revolvers. It was done as a reflex rather than a deliberation. McCallum looked over at his companion.

"Ready?"

Pedro nodded. "*Sí, jefe. Vamos.*"

The two men entered the dark passageway behind the hotel. It was long and unobstructed. Suddenly the Apache materialized as if he had just passed right through the wall. The two were startled and both took a step back. The Apache said nothing.

Thad was the first to speak. "You have the information we seek?"

The Indian nodded. "Some of my people and a few Yaquis I know have seen the large group of Mexicans you seek. They travel to the south of us."

"Can you show us exactly where they are?" Pedro asked. "As I said, we will pay you for your troubles."

The Apache considered the offer for a moment, then nodded.

"I will ride with you until the Mexicans you seek are found. No more."

McCallum smiled. "We'll leave first thing in the morning. Let's say we meet over at the livery stable."

"It will be so," the Apache replied. McCallum glanced over at Pedro who nodded his approval. When they turned back, the Indian was gone.

Chapter Twenty-Four

Standing in front of a line of three Dodge touring cars, Second Lieutenant George S. Patton addressed his first sergeant. "Ten men, correct?"

"Yes, sir, just as you requested," the sergeant replied.

"You bring Murphy along?" Patton asked.

The sergeant smiled. "Once I explained how he had no choice in the matter, he was glad to volunteer."

Patton chuckled. "Is he sober?"

"So far he is."

"Beats me where he finds the stuff."

"Well, sir, he may actually be making what he can't buy."

The lieutenant nodded. "There's one reason I want him along," he said, pointing at the cars. "If it is mechanical or electrical, Corporal Murphy can fix it, and these cars are both. I don't want to be caught out there in the middle of Chihuahua with a flat tire or a broken engine. Not with Villa's army running around."

"Maybe we should take more men?" the sergeant suggested.

"Might do so if we knew what we were up

against. But we don't. That's why the general requested just a small patrol to check out this ranch for signs of enemy activity. It'll probably end up being nothing, but if we encounter anything significant, we can always skedaddle on these fine mounts."

"If they're still running, that is," the sergeant joked. "Sir, what's the name of this place again?"

Lieutenant Patton pulled a map from his back pocket and spread it out on the hood of the first car. "Here it is, right here. A little way outside of Rubio. It's called the San Miguelito Ranch. Don't know much else about it. The locals claim to have knowledge of rebel activity in the vicinity."

"So, we're either the eyes or the bait?"

"You got that right, Sarge. By the way, how much ammo we got with us?"

"Every man has a sidearm and a rifle with thirty rounds apiece."

"Not a lot, but it should suffice," Patton commented.

"Well, sir, it's a funny thing about that. From what Corporal Murphy tells me, it seems that one of the cars has a spare case of .30-40 Krag rounds in the trunk and a crate of dynamite sticks."

"Is that so?" Patton asked.

"Yes, sir. Apparently, someone at the motor pool must have confused the boxes with the ones their tools come in. Does the lieutenant want me to send them back?"

Patton chuckled. He knew how the Army and its non-coms worked. Things tended to appear and disappear from time to time, depending on the whim of the men in charge. And contrary to popular belief that wasn't the top brass, it was the non-commissioned officers.

"No, it's probably just an honest mistake," Patton said. "Don't see as there's any sense in making the motor pool officer look bad. Especially not because of a simple oversight."

The sergeant smiled again. "I knew the lieutenant would feel that way. The stuff is in your lead car. The others are carrying extra water canteens and rations."

"Get everyone mounted up, Sergeant," Patton ordered. "I'll ride up front with Murphy and one of the guides. You take the next car and have the other civilian ride with you. The rest of the men will divide up evenly in all three vehicles." Glancing down at the Dodge car, he kicked a tire and muttered: "I still wish we were mounted on thoroughbreds."

Chapter Twenty-Five

It had been quite a while since Jeff had been kept under guard during the day. After all this time, General Villa was certain there was no way the *gringo* could escape by himself and he knew none of his men would ever risk betraying him. Besides, the *gringo* posed no threat to himself or his army. It stood to reason, therefore, that there was no sense in wasting resources guarding him closely.

Jeff Shaw, however, spent every waking moment planning an escape for himself and Mercedes. He knew he would have no weapon unless Mercedes managed to obtain an extra pistol or rifle for him. Even if she did, their only chance of successfully escaping lay in quickly putting as much distance between themselves and the *hacienda* as possible. The trick would be to get a head start.

Jeff had determined the best way to do that was to create a diversion. If it were big enough, it might buy them the time necessary to make good their escape. But what kind of diversion could he make?

Then, while stowing his camera equipment after another one of the general's requests for a photograph, Jeff accidentally spilled one of the developing chemicals. That little mistake was relatively inconsequential except for the fact that it reminded him of the time he had made a similar error at the shop and started a fire. Although it had been a small one, the fire had been difficult to extinguish because water didn't help. In fact, water seemed to make it worse. He remembered that his uncle had scattered some sort of powder over it, which had snuffed it out.

Jeff searched through the photography supplies, hoping he had the chemical in the wagon. If he could start a fire, he could use that as a diversion. Maybe he could even create a small explosion. But he would have to time the reaction so he could be away from the wagon when it went off. And then he would need time to meet up with Mercedes before all hell broke loose.

Creating the diversion became all he could think about. Once he had devised the outline of a plan, he was ready to discuss it with Mercedes. She suggested using the powder to create a trail of burn fuse once he had explained the chemical's flammable properties. The question was how to keep the powder from being noticed or scattered or extinguished by men, animals, or the natural elements once it was in place. Using a fuse of some sort seemed a good idea, but Jeff knew that he needed to come up with something else. After Mercedes departed, he worked on figuring out some other method.

He laughed to himself when he realized the solution had come to him in a flash. As he was checking the camera, his eyes settled on the cable to the mechanism that triggered the camera. If he could rig the trigger to some sort of battery or something that would create a spark, it might just do the trick. All he had to do was splice together some longer wire to create an electrical ignition rather than a wick or powder fuse.

Jeff spent the afternoon testing his trigger idea. He would use the chemicals to wet down the wagon bed. At the very least, the wood of the wagon would ignite, providing a small diversion. But if his idea of using a trigger was successful, the chemicals would create a large flash or possibly even an explosion, and the fire would burn hot and be hard to extinguish.

Next, Jeff began to consider how long to make the trigger mechanism. He knew he would have to be far enough away from the wagon so he wouldn't be hurt, but close enough to assure its success. Since the trigger didn't rely on combustion, he could bury the cable and it would still work. But he would have to make sure that no part of the cable was visible. If it were discovered, yanked free, or cut, their chance of escape would drop to zero.

Still, the biggest impediment to their escape as far as Jeff was concerned was Julio Cardenas and his obsession with Mercedes. There was really no telling when or if they would have a chance to try their plan.

• • •

An opportunity arose the very next day. When he returned to his wagon after washing up and getting coffee, Mercedes came to tell him that Cardenas and several of his closest allies had just ridden out for the day and weren't expected back until late that night, at the earliest. After discussing what they would need to do, step by step, they agreed to meet behind the stable after Jeff triggered the explosion. Mercedes promised she would have everything ready for them.

After making sure that no one was paying attention to him, Jeff used the leg of the tripod to burrow a small trench several inches deep in the soft dirt between the wagon and a tree a short but sufficient distance away to protect himself when he caused what he hoped to be an explosion. He walked back and forth, dragging the tripod leg, two more times between the wagon and the tree, before playing out the cable and kicking dirt over it to hide it.

Finally, after inspecting his work to ensure that nothing would seem out of the ordinary to the casual observer, he buried the trigger mechanism in the brush behind the tree, and went for a walk.

The afternoon seemed to drag on forever. Over and over, Jeff ran through scenarios in his head that could hinder the plan as he walked around. He felt certain luck was on their side since Cardenas was away from the *hacienda*.

Chapter Twenty-Six

The night had been a restless one for Thad McCallum. He was unaccustomed to the notion of failure, but it seemed he was no closer to finding his friend's son. Even if they did find the lad, McCallum had no plan for freeing him from the army that had seized him. If Jeff Shaw were even still alive that is.

After a fitful sleep, he awoke and dressed. Thad had a morning routine that continued even after his retirement from the Army. It included everything from stretching exercises, to the order he put on his clothes. He felt most comfortable when he could carry out his everyday routine, no matter where he was.

When he was fully dressed, he squared off in the hotel room's mirror and put on his old campaign hat. As a final gesture before leaving the room to join Pedro, he carefully checked his sidearm and rifle, then he took a deep breath, and went downstairs.

The two men stopped at the small restaurant that was located just off the lobby on the first floor and had a cup of coffee. Neither wanted to waste much time on a big breakfast, so McCallum dropped a few coins on the counter while Pedro grabbed a few of the sweet cakes on display.

They weren't as sugary as the donuts served up north, but they were soft and warm and went well with their morning coffee.

When McCallum and Pedro showed up at the livery, their horses had already been saddled and were ready to go. The Apache Skinyea was mounted, silently waiting for the pair. The two mounted, and the trio rode out.

"Talkative sort, ain't he?" Thad commented to Pedro after several hours of riding.

"Must not have anything to say," his friend replied, chuckling.

"Let's just hope he knows where he's going and isn't leading us out into an ambush," Thad said, then lit the tobacco in his pipe.

The three men traveled for the better part of three days without seeing any sign of Villa's army, or anyone of interest. On the third night, the men made camp under a large oak tree. McCallum was cleaning his plate of refried beans when he turned to Skinyea. McCallum's displeasure was more than apparent.

"How much farther do you reckon we have to go before we find Villa and his men? I'm getting a little tired of just riding around this god-forsaken country on a wild-goose chase."

"Not his fault, *jefe*," Pedro offered.

"Well, let him answer the question, anyway," McCallum said sharply.

"White men never did learn the virtue of patience," Skinyea replied.

McCallum tipped his hat back. "That's probably true, but didn't you ever learn to answer a direct question with a helpful answer?"

"One more day, maybe two," Skinyea said emphatically.

McCallum seemed skeptical. After a moment, Pedro asked how he knew this.

Skinyea looked at the two men and replied: "Many years ago, my people roamed the Southwest, on both sides of the Río Bravo. We owned this land. Then the Mexicans declared war on us. They did horrible things to our women and killed many of our children. The white men came next and fought us, too. Finally, they got together with the Mexicans and divided our land along the river. The thing is, they decided this without asking the Apaches. It was our land and we weren't even asked to take part in the talks. It was a treaty, as they say.

"Then it is the Americans on one side of the river and the Mexicans on the other. We fought for our people and our land. The white soldiers killed our chief, Mangas Coloradas, and cut off his head. The great chief Cochise realized the futility of fighting a people who number more than the stars in the skies, and made peace.

"Some chiefs, like Geronimo, refused to join the peace agreement and continued to raid into

Mexico. They felt we had only made peace with the United States, not the Mexicans. The peace Cochise made was kept by his people. The problem was that whenever a white man was killed, regardless of who did it, the Apaches were still blamed. If horses were stolen, even if by another tribe, it was blamed on the Apaches.

"Some white men tried to act in a fair manner, but when every soldier was looking for glory and when every reporter lied, the few who were on our side were easily ignored by the rest."

McCallum nodded. "I know this and believe it. So, I ask you again, why do you help us and how do you know where Villa is?"

Skinyea threw some sticks into the fire. "You have no patience."

Pedro just nodded.

Skinyea shrugged. "My people are scattered. Your people put some of us on reservations to starve, while others fled south. Now many years have passed and we just try to survive as a people.

"I have been told by others how to find this Villa and his army and I know the land. I chose to help you because as unfair as the Americans have been to us, the Mexicans have been worse, and I do not wish to have them succeed in ruining another family."

"That it?" McCallum asked.

Skinyea shook his head. "Unlike what many

have been told, we are not a heartless people when it comes to the innocent. This boy you spoke of has a sick mother and that is a good reason to find him. I loved my mother and would not like to think of her sick and worrying over me."

McCallum looked over at the guide. "Sorry, *amigo*. I want you to know we appreciate any help we can get." Pedro nodded in agreement.

"Besides," Skinyea put it, "I need the money."

Chapter Twenty-Seven

The sky was particularly dark that night. The moon was obscured by clouds and there were few stars out for that time in May. As far as Jeff Shaw was concerned conditions couldn't have been better. He would have checked his pocket watch but it had been taken by one of the Mexicans when they had first crossed the border. At the time, Jeff had been in no position to argue. He would just have to guess the hour.

Earlier he had met with Mercedes one last time to go over any last-minute concerns.

"Why did Cardenas ride out?" Jeff had asked.

"Villa ordered him to meet with another group that might want to join him," she had explained.

"Great. That's one less thing to worry about."

Mercedes had shaken her head. "We still need to worry. Julio is very . . . how you say? . . . unpredictable."

Jeff put his hands on her shoulders and stared into her eyes. "You want to change your mind? I can always go it alone." He couldn't believe what he was saying.

"*Querido*, you wouldn't get a mile by yourself."

"I'm not saying I want to, but I guess I would understand if you wanted to stay. We're taking a big chance. Gambling our lives."

"I no longer want to ride with these men," Mercedes insisted. "They are not what *la revolución* was supposed to be about. Besides, where you go now, I go," she added in a firm voice.

"Then tonight it is." Jeff looked around to make sure no one was watching, then kissed her quickly.

When he judged it was time to move ahead with the plan, Jeff went to the base of the tree where the trigger mechanism was hidden. He made sure no one was watching him, muttered a small prayer, and then triggered the mechanism he had constructed.

At first it didn't seem like anything was going to happen. Jeff was about to curse when he noticed the wagon bed was beginning to smoke. Maybe a minute passed by and then, suddenly, the wagon exploded in a huge ball of fire.

Jeff didn't look back as he ran straight toward the stable to meet with Mercedes. He found her outside the building with two saddled horses. She had just pulled her revolver from its holster, opened its cylinder, and checked that it was loaded and ready. Done, she glanced in Jeff's direction, and opened one of the saddlebags, pulling out another holster with a Remington single-action pistol in it. She tossed it to Jeff who wasted no time in buckling it on.

"Where did you get this?" he asked.

"I found the saddle in the back of the barn and the holster was inside the saddlebag. I think it belonged to *Señor* Richardson. The horse belonged to the *hacienda* as well. None of the soldiers has claimed it yet, so, if we are lucky, no one will even know that it is missing."

"Except us, that is."

Mercedes's expression became even more serious. "*Sí*, no one except us."

Jeff bent over and kissed her on the cheek before mounting. There was another large explosion at the other end of the *hacienda* as Mercedes mounted her horse. "Follow me quietly until we approach the gate. Then stay back in the shadows till I call for you," she cautioned.

The two had gone over this part of the plan carefully. If they could not get through the back gate without calling attention to themselves, then all their hopes would end right here.

Nervously, Mercedes and Jeff rode toward the gate. They could see the flames reaching up toward the treetops and getting dangerously close to the main house.

"Wait here," Mercedes whispered as she put a quirt to her horse and rode out into the open. As she neared the gate, she reined in her horse and started waving her arms and yelling. Jeff understood most of what she was saying.

"Hurry!" she yelled. "*El general*, he needs you. Didn't you hear the explosion?"

"But we were told to watch this gate," one of the guards protested.

"¡*Idioto*!" she yelled. "We may be under attack. General Villa will need everyone to fight. I will watch the gate till he orders you back. Go now. Go fight the fire before we lose the whole *hacienda*!"

The two soldiers had recognized Mercedes and knew her status with both General Villa and Captain Cardenas. It would be a toss-up as to whom the two men feared more. There was no reason to argue with her, especially if they were under attack. The pair hesitated only a moment, and then took off at a run.

Once the soldiers were out of sight Mercedes brought her horse right alongside the gate, and then reached down and undid the latch. She looked off into the darkness and whistled. "Now, Jeff, come, we ride," she muttered to herself.

Jeff Shaw came out from behind the trees, and, with Mercedes right behind him, the two galloped through the gate and away toward freedom and what they hoped would be a whole new life.

Chapter Twenty-Eight

Before the night was over Skinyea reminded them again that he would help McCallum and Peralta locate the Mexicans, not fight them. McCallum said he understood, but he felt regret that the Apache would not be staying on with them.

Neither Skinyea nor McCallum was the talkative sort; in fact, quite the opposite. Riding out on the trail for long periods quickly creates either an irritating annoyance between trail partners or a sense of camaraderie. In their case, it was camaraderie.

McCallum had always admired people who excelled at a specific skill, regardless of what it was, and in the short time they had ridden together, McCallum realized he had never met a finer tracker or anyone who could live off the land as well as Skinyea.

Admittedly, McCallum knew he could be stubborn and bossy. What retired sergeant wasn't? But his long friendship with Pedro surmounted any annoying personality traits. In fact, after all these years, the two men complemented each other. Pedro and Thad had ridden together for so long, they knew each other's moods, traits, and habits, good and bad. Pedro could read Thad like

213

a book and knew when to break the mood and when to shy away.

In many ways, the Apache Skinyea had fit in well with the two partners. He was forthright, honest, and extremely capable. Both McCallum and Pedro felt sure the Apache would have been an asset in any confrontation, but they understood his unwillingness to involve himself further in a problem that wasn't his.

After making camp on the following evening, the three men sat around their small fire, comfortably silent. Pedro smoked a cigarette he had rolled, and Skinyea slowly drank something he had brewed, using a concoction of herbs that he carried in a small leather pouch. McCallum puffed away on his pipe and from time to time sucked on some licorice. Thad offered the Apache a piece of the candy, but Skinyea immediately made a face and spit it out.

Pedro smiled since it was the only time he had seen the Apache change his expression since they had first met. McCallum chuckled as well. He had read once that some Indian tribes didn't like the taste of sweets and wondered if certain bands of Apaches were among them.

Thad wasn't offended because he had long ago learned that there were many people who didn't like the taste of licorice. Hell, if it weren't for his dyspepsia, it wouldn't be his first choice for a treat, either.

The next morning, McCallum and Peralta had awakened to find Skinyea was already up and about. His horse was saddled and, in fact, looked as though he had already been ridden hard.

"You've been out riding already?" Thad asked as Pedro built up the fire to heat coffee.

Skinyea merely nodded.

"So, did you find anything?" McCallum asked, frustrated that Skinyea seemed unwilling to supply any information beyond a nod of his head.

"I found many tracks to the southeast. It is about a two-hour ride," the Apache finally reported. "I will leave you now. You will find what you are seeking if you head in a straight line that way." He pointed to indicate the direction in which they should travel. "You are both good men. I wish you luck with your search."

McCallum looked over at Pedro, who shrugged. It was obvious by his expression that Thad was concerned about paying for the Apache's services before he could confirm that they would find Villa.

"Might as well pay him, *jefe*," Pedro said, reading his friend's mind. "So far on this trip he has been dead-on right about everything he's told us. No?"

"Yeah, I guess so," McCallum replied. Turning to the Apache, he said: "I trust you, Skinyea." McCallum reached into his pocket and pulled out a roll of Yankee greenbacks. "There's something extra in there. Pedro and I feel you deserve it." He handed Skinyea the money. "That said, we haven't actually found anyone yet."

"You will before today is over," Skinyea said confidently. "If not, come to the same place we first met and I will give you back your money. *Adiós*." Without another word, the Apache mounted his horse and galloped away.

Now it was Thad's turn to shrug. "Mighty sure of himself, ain't he?"

"Must be a reason for it," Pedro replied. "So, let's finish this coffee before it gets cold and then head out."

McCallum poured himself a cup of java, arching his stiff back before putting the coffee back on the fire. He looked off in the direction in which Skinyea had ridden. "I'm gonna miss that son-of-a-bitch, ya know."

Pedro nodded. "Me, too, but look on the bright side, *jefe*."

"Yeah, what's that?"

"You still got me for company," Pedro replied, smiling.

McCallum grunted. "Some bright side."

Chapter Twenty-Nine

When Julio Cardenas and his men returned to the *hacienda*, they found the place in a commotion. Men were running about with shovels and pails, yelling instructions at one another. There was a large fire spreading out in the area where the *gringo*'s wagon normally sat. The flames seemed to flare up with each attempt to douse it with water. Of course, Cardenas could see a few of the men—the naturally lazy ones— standing back, doing nothing, using the fire as an excuse to abandon their stations.

"*¿Que chingaos? ¿Que pasa aquí?*" he demanded angrily from horseback.

Looking up at the returning captain, one of the nearby soldiers replied that the *gringo*'s wagon had exploded.

"He was in it I hope," Cardenas hissed.

The soldier, fearful of incurring his captain's famous anger, cautiously answered: "We do not know yet. The fire is not yet out, and it is still so hot we cannot get close enough to see what remains. The general wanted us to make sure the fire did not spread to the main house."

Cardenas spurred his mount and quickly rode over to the house where Villa had established his headquarters. After dismounting, he practically ran inside.

"Where is the general?" he yelled at one of the men in the hallway.

The soldier pointed to the door leading to the *hacienda*'s library, then saluted. Without returning the salute, Cardenas pushed through the door and approached General Villa, who was seated behind a large oak desk, smoking a cigar. He looked up when Julio entered the room.

"*¿Que paso, Capitán?*" Villa asked.

"Have you seen Mercedes recently, *mi general?*" Cardenas asked impatiently.

Villa looked annoyed. "Business before pleasure, Julio. I meant how did your mission go?"

Cardenas became even more irritated. Still, Julio was no fool, so when Pancho Villa asked a question, Cardenas knew it had to be answered.

"It went very well, sir. Morales has finally agreed to join us. His men should arrive in a week or two. He has about two hundred men that he can gather together. And he confirmed what we have heard about the *gringo* army having invaded our country."

"*Excelente.* Good job. Soon then we will replenish our numbers. We lost too many after that last encounter with the *federales.*" Villa stood and laughed. "As for the *gringos* finding us . . . I wish them luck. You can go," he said.

"Sorry to interrupt you for a minute more, *mi general*, but I wish to know if you have seen Mercedes since the fire started?" Cardenas asked anxiously.

"No, I have not. I have had other things to worry about, you know."

"How about the *gringo*?"

"I haven't seen him, either. We believe the *pendejo* blew himself up while mixing his chemicals. The men say the fire is very hot. We cannot be sure about the *gringo* until the fire is under control." As an afterthought, Villa asked: "Why, what are you getting at?"

"I'm not sure, *mi general*, but I am wondering whether this was really an accident. Perhaps the *gringo* set the fire himself."

"Impossible. Why would he? What good would it do him? He has no horse, no gun. Besides, he has no idea where he is. There is no way he would even try to escape."

"Unless he had help," Cardenas suggested.

Pancho Villa thought for a moment, and then broke out laughing.

"Now I understand why you asked about Mercedes. You think she might have something to do with this?"

"I honestly don't know, but I am going to find out."

General Villa considered what Cardenas was suggesting for a moment. "Look for her. Begin here in the *hacienda*, and then search the camp. Find her. If, after an hour, you cannot locate her, take three or four men and go after them."

Cardenas nodded. "*Sí, mi general.*" He then turned to leave.

"One more thing, Julio."

Cardenas turned back.

"Know this, *Capitán*," Villa warned. "If that girl has betrayed us, the consequences will be a firing squad. Even if she is your woman."

"If she has betrayed me, I will shoot her myself," Cardenas replied. Just before he walked out the door, he added: "But first I will kill the *gringo*."

It was a half an hour of searching for Mercedes before Julio finally worked his way to the back gate. Finding it unattended, he ordered the guards tasked with the job brought to him. It took a while to find the two.

"Why did you abandon your post?" Cardenas shouted when they were brought to him.

The two looked at each other, confused.

The shorter of the two replied: "No, *mi capitán*, we did not abandon our station. We would never do so. No, *señor*, we were ordered to leave."

Julio slapped his leg with his riding crop, waiting for one of them to continue.

After a long pause, the taller of the two men, sweat beading on his forehead, explained:

"*La Señorita* Mercedes rode up and told us that *El General* Villa needed our help . . . in case we were being attacked. She said she would guard the gate until we were ordered to return."

"That is true, *Capitán*. I swear it," the shorter man added.

"*Maldita mentirosa*," Cardenas swore. "You two men stay here now, and if you leave this gate again, I will personally see you are hung for disobeying a direct order. But first I will rip off your balls. ¿*Comprende*?"

Terrified, the two soldiers hurried to their posts.

Turning to the men who had been helping him search for Mercedes, Cardenas ordered: "The rest of you get your horses, guns, and plenty of ammunition. Be back here as fast as you can." Reconsidering, Cardenas barked: "Make that two horses for each man! All saddled and ready to go. We will have a hard ride ahead of us, I think. ¡*Andale muchachos*! ¡*Vamanos*!"

Chapter Thirty

After riding through a good part of the night, Jeff Shaw and Mercedes pulled up their horses for a rest. "We will stop here," Mercedes said, wiping her forehead with a small rag of a handkerchief.

"You sure we can take the risk?" Jeff asked. He looked around nervously.

"Our horses need a break. Without them, we will not make it," Mercedes replied. "We have pushed them as hard as we can. Luckily for us, the horses of the men who will be chasing us will get just as worn out. Even if they are only a couple of hours behind us, that provides us with at least an hour for our mounts to rest. They won't catch us. Either they rest, too, which gives us time, or they run their horses to death."

"I guess that makes sense," Shaw agreed. "But I'm still gonna keep watch while you get some sleep."

"*De acuerdo*," Mercedes replied, nodding. "But I will make you some coffee first, *querido*. It will put something in your stomach and help keep you from dozing off."

"All right," he said. "Just as long as you get a little rest."

She smiled at him as Jeff loosened their saddle

cinches before leading the horses over to a nearby pool of water to allow them to drink. As he passed her, she leaned over and touched his arm gently.

"Do you think I will like your home in America?" she asked.

"I think so," Jeff responded. "It's not nearly as hot and dry there as it is here."

"Do you think your family will approve of me?" Mercedes asked shyly.

"I think they will adore you," Jeff replied sincerely. "They will love you as much as I do." He kissed her on the forehead, then added: "Just don't wear the pistol when you say hello to my mother." Jeff laughed, and Mercedes punched him playfully in the shoulder. It felt good to forget the danger they were in for a few minutes.

Jeff sipped coffee from time to time while pondering how often life makes a complete turn. One moment he is in a shop learning how to be an apprentice photographer, and the next he is on the run from an army of Mexican revolutionaries. And after his time with the *Villaistas*, he knew that if Villa's men were to catch up with him, he would be shot. If Julio Cardenas didn't torture and kill him first, that is. As for what Julio would do to Mercedes, he refused to let his mind even consider that.

The two had rested for a couple of hours before getting back on the trail. Although there was no sign of pursuit yet, Jeff and Mercedes tried as much as possible to stay off the skyline, and they closely watched their back trail. When they could, they took advantage of rocky areas, which they hoped would slow any pursuit. Generally, they traveled northwest. Jeff now made sure they slowed and walked their horses for short periods.

"Where are we headed?" Jeff asked during one of these breaks to cool the horses.

"There is a small *rancho* that is due . . . *oeste* . . . west. I have seen it several times in the past," Mercedes explained. "We should be able to rest and eat there before heading to Rubio. It is not that far."

"Rubio? And just what is that?" Jeff asked.

"It is one of the larger towns in the area. We may be able to find help there. If not, maybe someone there will be able to confirm whether troops from your country have entered Mexico. If that has happened, then we can try to find them, and learn the safest route to the border."

Shaw nodded. "But won't Villa be thinking the same thing? Maybe he will go straight to this Rubio place."

Mercedes shrugged. "*Tal vez*, but I think not."

"Why?"

"If we are lucky, they will think we are going straight *norte*. To the border."

"And why don't we, *querida*?" Jeff asked. "It does make sense, doesn't it?"

Mercedes shook her head. "No, it is too obvious. I am counting on them thinking that. They will send patrols to cut us off, I think. Plus, we would never make it that way. These horses would give out long before we reached the Río Bravo. And our supplies are few."

"We're still deep in Mexico. Doesn't that mean Villa controls everything around here?"

Mercedes smiled. "It may seem that way when you are with him, but no. You forget that Francisco Villa is a *revolucionario*, a rebel. The government still controls most of the country. Especially the large towns. And if your army has invaded, Villa is losing much popularity with the people."

"So why don't we just find an army group, or police? What do you call them . . . *federales*? Aren't they out on patrol? Maybe they would help us."

Mercedes shook her head. "You forget one thing."

Jeff cocked his head. "Yeah? What's that?"

"Look how I am dressed. I was a *revolucionaria*, too. The *federales* are not very forgiving of rebels."

Jeff frowned. "So, no help there, eh?"

"I am afraid not, *querido*."

Shaw thought for a moment, looked at Mercedes, and smiled. "Then for now, it's just you and me." He started to remount his horse.

"So, we might as well ride to this *ranchero* of yours."

"*Rancho*," she corrected after she, too, had mounted her horse. "Yes, just us two. You know, *gringo*," she said, smiling, "I think I really do love you."

Jeff Shaw looked over at her. "Think? Hell, I know it. So, what do you say? Let's ride."

Chapter Thirty-One

Some people might have taken the time to consider various options before undertaking such a pursuit. The captain, however, was not a cautious or pragmatic man, but rather the opposite. He was impulsive, impatient, and, at the present, furious. The thought that someone he considered to be his woman had taken off with another man infuriated him. The thought that it was that miserable little *gringo* sent him into a complete rage.

Cardenas was not about to take the time to consider his options. Mercedes had ridden out the west gate, so, dammit, he was riding west right behind her, with his closest allies. And he was riding hard and fast.

Still, Cardenas was no fool. Julio knew that with Mercedes's head start, he would need an advantage if he was to have any hope of catching up with her. That was why he had ordered his men to bring spare horses.

And he was being ruthless with his men. After several hours of hard riding, he ordered his men to do a *paso de la muerte*, or pass of death in English. It is an old *vaquero* phrase for a dangerous maneuver in which the rider jumps from his horse onto another horse that is running alongside. By switching to the relatively fresh mounts and releasing the ones that the men had been riding, Cardenas could almost double the distance they could travel in the same time frame.

By 8:00 a.m. the captain and his men came across the campsite where Mercedes and Jeff had stayed.

"It is only two or three hours old, *mi capitán*," one of the men indicated. Knowing this man's skills at tracking and reading sign, Cardenas had ordered him to dismount and inspect the site. "We are catching up. At this rate, we may find them by noon," the tracker added.

Cardenas looked over at the small pool of water and ordered the rest of his men to dismount. "Cool your horses off, and then water them. Fill your canteens and check your weapons. We ride in fifteen minutes, no more."

The captain looked to the horizon and grinned wickedly. "I will catch you, *gringo*, and then I will cut off your *cojones* and stuff them in your mouth."

As they were preparing to leave, the tracker spoke up. "*Capitán*, I believe I know where they are headed."

"Where?" Cardenas asked.

"There is a *rancho* called San Miguelito that is not all that far from here. It is in the direction in which they are headed. I know it well. There are no other such places around here to rest or get help."

Cardenas grinned with satisfaction. "*Bueno.* San Miguelito, it is then. We know where we are headed. But, all of you, keep your eyes open for any sign that they may have changed direction. And," he added to the tracker, "if you are wrong, I will do to you what I have planned for them."

The man gulped and nodded seriously. "*Sí, Capitán.* It must be the place, but I will make sure I do not lose their trail."

"*Mas te vale,*" Cardenas warned. In English, it meant "you'd better."

Knowing the pair's destination made it easier and faster to follow them. There was no reason to constantly stop to verify their trail. Before the fifteen minutes were up, Julio Cardenas ordered his tracker on ahead. Remounting several minutes later, he and the the two other men followed at a gallop.

Cardenas felt confident that by the end of the day he was going to get the satisfaction he had wanted since the first time he had encountered that *gringo*.

Meanwhile, although they were hopeful of having made a clean get-away, Jeff Shaw and Mercedes Valdez de Guerrera were riding as if the hounds of hell were on their tails.

"How long till we get to this ranch?" Jeff shouted over to Mercedes.

Mercedes looked around and reined her horse back from a gallop into a fast jog. "It should only be about an hour or two away. I think we will make it safely to San Miguelito."

Jeff slowed and pulled his horse up alongside hers. "Sure hope you're right, sweetheart."

"Our horses are tiring," she advised him.

"Do you think we can exchange our horses for fresh ones at this Miguel place?" Shaw asked.

"Rancho de San Miguelito," she reminded him again. "*Sí*, I believe so, but if not, at least it is a place where we can rest them a while, get water and food. Maybe someone there knows about the location of the American Army."

Jeff smiled. "Sounds good to me. I know you rode with Villa, but the sooner and the farther away we get from him and his army, especially his boy Julio, the better I'll like it."

"I ride with you now, *mi amor*, and am happy to do so." Then she added: "But if we ever do meet up with Julio, I wouldn't let him hear you refer to him as a boy."

Jeff considered what Mercedes had said. "If we do meet up with him again, I doubt either one of us will live long enough to apologize for the insult." Then as they dismounted to walk their horses, he asked her how she ever came to be associated with someone like Julio Cardenas.

Mercedes thought for a few moments before replying. "When I was younger, I lived with my family in a small town outside of San Luis Potosi. My papa ran a small saddle shop in the town, but just about everything was owned by the *alcalde* . . . the mayor . . . and his son, José Padilla. I was just a girl when José Padilla started showing an interest in me. I was studying with the *cura*, the priest, at the mission school. That is where I learned English."

"Must have been a pretty good teacher if you ask me," Jeff observed.

"He was. Anyway, José wanted my papa to promise me to him in marriage. He owned the building where my papa's shop was and threatened to close the shop when Papa could not pay the higher rent he was demanding. My papa loved me dearly, but he had my mama and brothers to worry about, too, and was being pressured all the time by this man. My papa became desperate. He asked me to at least consider the offer of marriage, but I said José was too old for me and I did not love him. I was very afraid because it is the custom to allow the father of a young girl to decide on who was to be her husband."

"So, what did you do and how does Cardenas fit in?" Jeff asked.

"Well, I soon realized I had no choice in the

matter. But I could not and would not marry such an awful man."

"Yet you became involved with Cardenas?" Jeff was trying to understand.

Mercedes gave him a look that made him realize the stupidity of his question. "He did not appear so at first."

"Sorry, that was wrong of me to say. Go on," he apologized.

"I got help from the people at the mission against their better judgment. They gave me supplies and a horse and I fled away from the village. I was on the trail for what seemed like a very long time. I wanted to go to La Ciudad de Mexico . . . Mexico City, as you call it . . . but after a week or so I was out of food and very scared. Also, my horse was becoming lame. Then one day a band of riders approached. I feared for my life. A woman alone on the trail is never safe."

"Especially around those men," Jeff observed.

"I lived with those men for years. Please try to understand."

Jeff nodded. "I'm trying, but you are so sweet, I have trouble making the connection."

"When the men rode up, the leader took one look at my condition and offered me his arm and pulled me up behind him on his saddle. He ordered the rest to leave me alone."

"Let me guess . . . Julio Cardenas."

"*Sí*, and he was very respectful of me at first. He was also very powerful and all the men obeyed him and left me alone. He then introduced me to *el caudillo*."

"Pancho Villa?" Jeff inserted.

"*Sí*, yes," Mercedes replied. "And he began to talk of *la revolución* and his vision for the future of our country. He can be a very inspiring and convincing man, and I became a follower. I believed in what he said, but, truthfully, as hard as it may be to believe, I think that even though I was living with rebels and taking part in dangerous raids, I felt safe and alive. How could that not be better than being alone on the trail?"

"I get that. Obviously, I know the feeling."

"But over time both Pancho and Julio have changed," Mercedes explained. "You see, at first we had great victories and everything was good, but then the government men in power made deals, and money became harder to come by. An army needs money for supplies, and we had less and less."

"So, what happened?" Jeff asked.

"Well, we began to lose battles and the men became angered."

"And Julio?"

"At first I thought he was kind and considerate, but I began to realize that he was simply being protective of me because he considered me to be his property. Also, both Pancho and Julio began to enjoy the battles more and more. They became more . . . what is the word . . . ?"

"Bloodthirsty?" Jeff replied.

"*Sí*, very bloodthirsty, very vicious. Julio seems to enjoy pushing around his soldiers and making them fear him. I know I am more afraid of him now than I was when I first met him."

"And then I came along?" Jeff asked.

Mercedes smiled. "*Sí, mi amor.* Then you came along."

"You do know that I would never treat you badly or hurt you like he does, don't you?"

Mercedes tapped her pistol and laughed. "You'd better not!"

Chapter Thirty-Two

Stop the car, Corporal Murphy," Patton ordered. He held his arm outside the car window, just as he would if on a horse-mounted patrol. The two motorcars behind them quickly came to a stop.

The sergeant got out of the second car along with his guide.

"Ten-minute break, Sergeant," Patton ordered. "If the men've got to answer the call of nature, now's the time to do so."

The sergeant grinned. "Yes, sir." He turned to the men getting out of the two cars to the rear as they stretched, not used to being cooped up in a car. "You heard the man. Piss break. And water up if you have to, but make sure you get it done in ten minutes."

Patton laughed to himself and began spreading his map over the hood of his command car. He gestured for the two civilians to approach. What do you think?" he asked them.

"About forty-five minutes to the ranch, I reckon," one of the two men replied. The other, who was looking over their shoulders, began to nod in agreement.

"Thank you," Patton replied. "Take ten before we ride on."

The lieutenant reached into the Dodge to retrieve a pair of binoculars that were inside on the seat. Patton used the field glasses to survey the horizon, then handed the instrument to the sergeant. "See anything that looks like *bandidos*, Sarge? Anything out of the ordinary?"

The soldier took the binoculars and scanned the surroundings. After a few moments of studying the landscape, he shook his head. "Hell, Lieutenant, your eyes are as good as mine. Better probably, but I don't see anything, either."

"Damn," Patton griped. "I was hoping to run into a few of the bastards. It's about time we got a chance to grab 'em by the nose and kick 'em in the pants."

The sergeant shrugged. "I suppose there's nothing wrong with just riding around all day in a nice comfortable car, and then going home without getting shot at."

Patton shook his head. "You never get ahead in this man's Army by playing it safe, Sergeant. Remember . . . *'L'audace, l'audace, toujours l'audace!'*"

The sergeant looked at him, not understanding. "Sorry, sir, but I don't speak no Mex."

Patton smiled. "It's not Spanish, it's French. Fredrick the Great first said it. It means 'Audacity, audacity, always audacity.' One of the benefits of a West Point education, Sergeant."

The sergeant, while an expert in combat, was a

man who probably couldn't even spell audacity. He looked back blankly at his commanding officer. "Audacity? Frederick the Great? Right, sir."

The sergeant glanced toward the patrol. "I think I'll get the men mounted up." He turned to the rest of the soldiers, shouting: "All right, you doughboys, everyone in the cars! Mount up! We're wasting daylight!"

Lieutenant Patton got back in his Dodge and turned to the corporal. "All right, Murphy, you know the way. Move out. Let's see if we can find us some damned *revolucionarios*."

Chapter Thirty-Three

If anything will get you killed, it is complacency and assumption. Once the Rancho de San Miguelito was in sight Mercedes and Jeff settled their horses into a walk. On the one hand, it made sense not to press the horses, but part of their rationale for walking them was the belief that Villa's men could never overtake them after so many hours on the trail.

"The *rancho*'s just ahead," Mercedes said, pointing off into the distance.

"You know, *querida*," Jeff said smiling, "I think you did it. I think we're going to make it, after all." The words were barely out of his mouth when a bullet whistled right by his ear.

"Damn," he swore. "What the hell?"

Mercedes glanced back over her shoulder in time to recognize Julio Cardenas and three, maybe four other riders galloping over the crest of the last hill she and Jeff had crossed.

"Ride, Jeff! Fast!" she screamed. "Head for the *rancho*!"

Shaw didn't need any encouragement. He spurred his horse into a full gallop right behind her. He may have been young, but he was no coward. He wanted to protect the woman he loved. If any rifle bullet was to going to hit someone, Jeff wanted to make sure it would be him, not her, so he did his best to shield her.

Off in the distance, less than a half a mile to the southwest, Thad McCallum and Pedro Peralta had heard the shots. Instinctively both men spurred their horses toward the sound of the gunfire. When they crested the next hill, the two men pulled to a stop as they saw the *hacienda*. Thad reached back into his left saddlebag and pulled out the pair of binoculars he had bought. He shook his head in disbelief. "It couldn't be!" he exclaimed. He stopped himself from taking out the picture of Jeff from his pocket for the time being.

"What is it, *jefe*?" Pedro asked.

"There's a pair running from some Mexicans. Looks like a man and a girl. And, if I'm not mistaken, the man looks to be American. As hard as it may be to believe it, we may have stumbled upon the lad we're looking for."

"Got to be him, *jefe*," Pedro observed. "How many *gringos* on the run are there this far south? He must have escaped from the *Villaistas*."

"Doesn't look like they've escaped just yet," McCallum replied grimly. "Those riders are catching up mighty quick. Here, look for yourself."

Thad handed the binoculars to Pedro. Down in the valley the pursuers were firing at the two from horseback.

After he took a look, Pedro handed the glasses back. "They'll make it to the ranch, I think, but they are going to need help once they get there."

"Well,"—Thad shrugged—"that's why we came." He quickly put the binoculars away and removed the thong from his holster. Pedro did the same. Both McCallum and Peralta dropped the ropes to the pack mules and pulled their rifles from their sheaths.

"On the count of three," McCallum said, adjusting the rear sight on his Winchester. Once Thad reached three, both men began firing from the crest of the hill. One of the Mexican rebels fell from his horse, forcing the others to rein in quickly. The fallen rider was helped back onto his horse.

At that distance neither Thad nor Pedro had expected to be lucky enough to hit anything. The best they had hoped for was to slow the pursuers down long enough for the pair in front to get to cover. It appeared they had been successful at that.

"Time to ride, my friend," Thad indicated, tightening the strap on his hat.

"One last time, *jefe*?" Pedro asked.

"Hell, I hope not." McCallum's voice rose with excitement. "All right, once more into the breach, Pedro!"

Peralta gave out a loud *vaquero* yell, and then both men charged down the hill.

Chapter Thirty-Four

You hear that?" Patton asked Corporal Murphy. Given the heat in that part of the country, the windows in the Dodges were rolled down. In fact, the lieutenant had been riding with his head sticking out the car window.

"Must be one of the cars backfiring, sir."

Patton looked over at him in disgust. "Bullshit. You know as well as I do those were gunshots."

The corporal shrugged. "If you say so, sir."

"Damned right I say so. All right, Murphy, ride straight toward the gunfire."

The lieutenant stuck his arm out the window, waving the other two cars on. "Follow us!" he yelled. Turning again to Murphy, he said: "Come on, give it all she's got, Corporal. Push her as fast as this metal contraption will go."

Bouncing along the road, if one could call it that, the three cars followed the sound of the gunfire. As they topped the hill, Patton had the cars come to a stop. He got out of the lead car and walked quickly back to the sergeant, who by this point had already exited his car. The two studied the ranch below.

"We are going to ride around to the back of the place, and then drive straight in," Patton explained. "As soon as we get inside the compound, I want everyone out, guns loaded. Spread out and use the cars for cover if you have to. Got it?"

"Yo!" replied the soldier.

The lieutenant returned to his automobile and watched the sergeant sprint back to the last car to give them the orders. After returning to his own car, Patton patted Corporal Murphy on the shoulder. "All right, Murphy, time to earn our pay. Drive on around behind the ranch."

As the Army's cars headed down the hill toward the ranch, McCallum and Peralta, were already galloping through the front gate. Both men slid their horses to a halt and jumped from their saddles at the same time. McCallum winced a little when his leg hit the ground. He was too energized to worry about the pain, but in the back of his mind he knew that his right hip would give him hell later.

"The two are in the house on the left, Pedro. Spread out!" McCallum yelled.

McCallum knew Peralta could read the situation as well as he could, but Thad wanted to make sure neither was hit unnecessarily by the crossfire of either friend or foe.

They started firing together as they ran toward the house. McCallum fired his Winchester repeatedly, levering it from the hip. Peralta carried his rifle in his left hand and had drawn his pistol and was thumbing it with his right hand.

"Americans coming in!" McCallum shouted, crashing his body through the door and into the house where the man and the woman were holding out. As the door crashed open, he could feel a sharp pain rack his left shoulder.

"God-damned rheumatism!" he cursed, thinking that his shoulder would be yet another part of his body that would be reminding him of his trip to Mexico once he made it home.

A girl turned and, aiming her pistol at the new arrivals, was about to shoot when Pedro entered and yelled in Spanish: "¡*Somos amigos*¡ ¡*No disparen*!"

Jeff stepped over to Mercedes's side and put his hand on her pistol, pushing it down. "Who are you?" he asked.

"Your name Shaw?" the American asked.

Both Jeff and Mercedes were shocked.

"Yes, sir, it is," Jeff replied.

A windowpane shattered, the glass exploding into the room. Pedro ran to the window and fired two pistol shots toward the attackers. He used the barrel of his gun to dislodge the remaining shards stuck in the window's frame, then, stooping, he settled his rifle through the opening.

McCallum quickly looked around the room and told Jeff and the girl to get down and stay away from the windows. He took a position at a window near Pedro, levering two rounds in succession. As he was doing so, he instinctively surveyed the yard and its structures.

The Mexicans had taken cover in two buildings adjacent to each other directly across from the house. Based on where the shots were coming from, McCallum guessed there were two men in each building. They were protected by solidly built walls and would be hard to hit and even harder to dislodge. Considering everything, he and Pedro had been lucky to get inside the house without being hit.

"*Mierda*," cursed Cardenas. "Where the hell did these two come from and who the hell are these *cabrones*?"

There was no answer from the rebel at his side.

"Reload faster!" Cardenas ordered. "I want those two dead."

As soon as Cardenas started firing, the other three Mexicans began shooting rounds into the house.

Inside, the three men and Mercedes were hunkering down as windows shattered and wood splinters flew around the room.

"Look on the bright side, *jefe*," Pedro shouted above the noise.

"What bright side?" Thad responded, ducking a shot. "What now?"

"Well, for one thing we found the *muchacho* alive."

Another round pounded into the wall behind McCallum as he glared at his friend. "Yeah, that he is. Or at least he is for now."

"We can shoot. Let us help you!" Jeff shouted above the firing.

McCallum shook his head violently. "We've come too far to see you get your head blown off. You stay down, or I'll shoot you myself. I promised I'd get you back to Maggie and that's what I aim to do."

At the mention of his mother's name Jeff stood up in surprise. A peppering of bullets broke through one of the windows and almost hit him, missing his head by mere inches.

"Damn if you ain't got the brains God gave a goat," McCallum commented. "Is there a part of stay the hell down that you don't comprehend? I swear someone must have beaten Al to the punch, 'cause you can't be his kid."

Jeff dropped down and covered Mercedes. "Who the hell are you?" he asked McCallum again. He was more puzzled than ever.

At that precise moment, they heard the motorcars roar through the back gate. They listened as the engines stopped to the south of the house, and the men exited the vehicles. Several minutes elapsed before they began shooting at the two structures where the Mexicans had holed up.

"Sounds like the cavalry has arrived, *jefe*," Pedro observed happily. No sooner had the words come out of his mouth than shots began being fired at the house, too.

McCallum stormed to the door and stuck his hat out. He quickly realized he would have to prove he was an American and on their side, or, in the heat of battle, they'd end up dead right along with the Mexicans.

"Stop shooting at us you flat-footed, limp, illegitimate sons of drunken Marines," he shouted when there was a pause in the shooting. "We're Yankees in here, god dammit! If you sons-of-bitches ever stopped playing with yourselves long enough to pass basic training, you'd know to shoot at the other buildings where the rebels are and leave us the hell alone. We're on your god-damned side!"

While Lieutenant Patton caught only some of the words McCallum was shouting, he knew they were coming from an American. He ordered his men to stop shooting at the house.

"Looks like we have at least one American civilian inside," he remarked to Corporal Murphy.

"From the sound of it, if he's a civilian now," Murphy observed, "he wasn't at some point in his life. Sounds more like a pissed-off drill sergeant to me, sir."

Patton grinned and fired a shot off at one of the outbuildings which held two of the rebels.

The patrol's sergeant crept over to Patton, sliding on his side next to him. "Those bastards are solidly under cover, sir. We're getting nowhere fast this way."

"You have something in mind, Sergeant?" Patton asked.

"Remember the dynamite sticks in the trunk, sir?"

Patton grinned again. He seemed to be enjoying himself. Turning to the civilian guides, Patton ordered them to stay put.

"Corporal Murphy, you go get the dynamite ready," he directed. "Sergeant, you get into that house somehow and tell them what we're planning to do. I'd suggest they join us as soon as the fireworks begin."

The sergeant looked at the space between the cars and the house where McCallum and the others were hiding out and grimaced. A volley of rifle fire was directed at the motorcars. "Yes, sir," he replied, swallowing with difficulty.

"We'll cover you. Stay low and run hard."

"No shit. As if I couldn't figure that one out . . . sir," the sergeant replied sarcastically.

"Hey, you in there, I'm coming in. Don't nobody shoot me!" the sergeant yelled as he began to propel himself across the open space between the car and the house. Patton's men started firing at the two outbuildings as soon as the sergeant had warned the house. Still, bullets from the Mexicans peppered the ground around him as he ran. He gained the porch, then crashed through the doorway that had been opened by someone inside, fell, and rolled. When he regained his feet, he was surprised to be looking at a fully armed Mexican. He steadied his gun.

Thad edged away from the window and warned: "Easy does it, Sarge. Pedro, there, is an American, too, and he's on our side."

The soldier was skeptical, but then seemed relieved. "What are you all doing here?" he asked.

Jeff Shaw was about to answer when McCallum beat him to it. "The lad is on the run from Villa's men. His pa's ex–regular Army. We're here to bring him home. I have no idea who the girl is."

Jeff looked up, surprised. "She's with me," he explained. Turning to McCallum, he repeated: "Who the hell are you, anyway?"

Thad ignored him for the moment. "What's the plan, Sarge?" he asked.

The sergeant recognized a commanding presence when he met one. Regardless of who these other folks were, it was obvious that the tall, older man was in charge. Pedro had returned to the window and was once again firing his rifle at the rebels.

"The lieutenant has decided to use dynamite to deal with the situation. It'll either kill them or bring them out in the open. So, as soon as it starts getting even noisier out there, we all bail and join him," the sergeant explained. Taking in the room, he asked: "Anyone else around here we need to know about?"

"Not as far as we can tell," McCallum answered, shaking his head. "The locals probably beat it the hell out of here as soon as they heard gunfire, or the place was abandoned before today. I count four of them shooting." He ducked as a rifle bullet slammed into the wall.

"I make it to be four, too, *jefe*," Pedro commented between shots.

"One of them is Julio Cardenas," Mercedes broke in. "He is one of Pancho Villa's captains. He is *muy malo*. A very dangerous man."

"A real hardcase, eh?" the sergeant said. "Well, we'll see how he handles some TNT. It shouldn't be too long before all hell breaks loose. Then we'll take off."

Thad gestured at the pair kneeling on the floor. "The sergeant and I go first, then you two follow, and I'd advise you to cling to us like flypaper. Pedro, you follow behind them, and try not to get your ass shot off."

Peralta smiled and nodded. "Same goes for you, *jefe*."

The sergeant had cracked open a small, side window where he had a view of the Dodge cars. The Army riflemen were shooting steadily at the opposite buildings, giving as good as they got.

He watched as Corporal Murphy pulled out a dynamite stick. Another soldier, one the sergeant recognized as Private O'Neill, lit it. As soon as that happened, the corporal threw it. He lit a second and third stick in quick succession and hurled them as hard as he could in the direction of the two outbuildings.

The first blast caused part of the front wall to cave in on the building on the left. When the second and third blasts went off, the sergeant gave the signal to run. The small group hurried through the door of the *rancho* as fast as they could. As the sergeant, Jeff, and Mercedes headed for the cover of the cars, McCallum and Peralta veered over to where Patton had positioned himself once the first stick of dynamite exploded.

Not surprisingly, Patton was the only one out in the open in front of the three vehicles. Standing erect and fearlessly, he was in the process of pulling cartridges from his gun belt.

"Come on out of there, you damned rebels and give yourselves the hell up!" he shouted, reloading his Colt pistol. He had barely glanced over when Thad and Pedro joined him, but now he addressed them: "Welcome to the party, boys."

"Hell of a party, *señor*," Pedro remarked.

The three stood there, awaiting a response from the damaged buildings.

"Reckon we got 'em?" Patton wondered aloud.

McCallum shrugged, saying: "I can't see how we couldn't have."

The three watched and waited for several minutes, the shooting having ceased. Slowly two figures coated with adobe dust emerged from the right-hand building. Then another staggered from the other structure, collapsing before taking ten steps out into the sunlight.

"Guess not," the lieutenant observed. Turning his head back to the cars, he ordered: "Hold your fire, men!" Then, in the direction of the *Villaistas*, he shouted: "Do you surrender?"

It occurred to both the men under Patton's command, as well as to Jeff Shaw, that the lieutenant and the two men next to him out in the open were crazier than hell.

But instead of surrendering, the two rebels bolted for their horses. As they attempted to mount, they fired at the Americans. In response, and almost as one, McCallum, Peralta, and Patton fired back. Both rebels fell to the ground. Their horses spooked and took off.

As the attention of the Americans was drawn by the escape attempt, Cardenas emerged from the right-hand building and whistled for his horse. By the time anyone noticed him, he was in the saddle.

McCallum and Patton raised their pistols at the same time, took aim, and fired. For a moment,

Pedro was not sure they had hit anything, but then Cardenas fell from his horse, face down, into the dirt. His horse took off as if chased by a lightning bolt.

The trio holstered their weapons, and then walked slowly toward the bodies. Pedro went to check on the man who had barely made it out of the building before collapsing. He was dead.

"Nice shooting, I'd say," Patton remarked. Thad glanced over at him. "Yours, not mine," the lieutenant added.

McCallum shrugged. "Pretty close, if you ask me, sir." It was a force of habit to always credit the officer in charge when success was achieved, but deep down he knew his shot had hit its mark.

Mercedes ran to Cardenas's body, and dropped to his side. Rolling his body over, she ran her hand over his face to clean it. He may have tried to kill her, but, still, they had once been lovers.

"It's Cardenas. Captain Julio Cardenas," Jeff explained as he walked over to Thad's side. "He's General Villa's right-hand man. Or at least he was," he said as he kept his eyes on Mercedes.

Patton looked over and studied the young man before addressing him. "If you and the girl came from Villa's camp, we need to talk to you about his whereabouts."

Having returned to the small group, Pedro responded before Jeff could even open his mouth. "Even if they told you, it wouldn't help. Once Villa hears about this, he and his men will be long gone."

No one contradicted him.

Thad saw the look on Patton's face, and decided to make introductions. "This is Pedro Peralta, my ranch foreman and friend, and my name is Thaddeus McCallum." It was a toss-up as to who was more surprised, Jeff Shaw, Lieutenant Patton, or his sergeant. The three looked over at McCallum as if they were looking at a ghost.

"You're my Uncle Thad?" Jeff asked. "I mean . . . are you my godfather?"

McCallum smiled and nodded. "Since I cleaned your ass once or twice when you were in diapers, I guess your pa thought I would be the logical one to pull it out of the fire now."

Patton was a keen student of history and his sergeant was old enough to have heard many stories about the Iron Sergeant when he was growing up. They both recognized McCallum's name.

"I thought you was dead," the sergeant said.

"Not hardly," McCallum growled. "Leastwise, not yet."

"The Iron Sergeant. Well, I'll be damned," Patton observed. "We can fit you folks in our cars and take you back to our base before we get reinforcements and go after Villa."

"More rust than iron, if you ask me,"

253

McCallum replied. His shoulder was getting stiff and beginning to throb. "Look, Lieutenant, if it's all right with you, I'd prefer to return the way I got here."

Patton's eyebrows arched. "It's not a problem. We can make room in the cars," Patton assured McCallum.

"Thanks, but that's not it, Lieutenant. You see, I know the Army and its red tape. I've been around Black Jack Pershing long enough to know what will happen if I show up there with these folks in tow."

Patton instinctively flinched a little at the mention of General Pershing's nickname. "I'm not sure I know what you mean," he said.

"First, I'll have to explain what the hell we are doing here, and then he'll have to fill out reports and we'll have to answer questions till the cows come home. Then we'll have to repeat it again in triplicate to his intelligence officers," Thad explained. "Army intelligence . . . well, I always thought there was something ironic about that title. Then after chewing my ass out for taking matters into my own hands, Pershing will probably want to reminisce about the good old days in Cuba."

"Knowing the general, I'd say that was about right," Patton agreed.

"Pedro and I just want to get back home to our ranch. I'm getting too old for all this horseshit."

The sergeant laughed loudly.

"I doubt that very much," Patton stated.

"If it's just the same to you, I'd prefer the report didn't even mention us. None of us was even here, if you get my drift. The glory is all yours."

The lieutenant considered Thad's last statement before finally nodding. Then: "Sergeant, these folks were never here," he advised. "Make sure the men know it. I'll make sure they get R and R when they get back, but if they even mention these people, they'll be doing latrine duty for a year. Make sure the civilian guides understand it, too. Tell them I'll personally make it worth their while."

"Yes, sir," the sergeant replied. Turning to the men, he yelled: "Put your rifles' safeties back on and prepare to move out!"

Pedro rounded up his horse and the black for McCallum before picking out two fresh mounts for Jeff Shaw and the girl. He made sure they had enough water, and then requested a few supplies from the soldiers. It was more than enough to get them to Rubio.

There were handshakes all around. "Thank you again, Lieutenant," McCallum said. "You might just go the distance in this man's Army."

Patton looked back at the older man and| smiled. "Coming from you that means a lot. I appreciate it." He threw McCallum a smart salute.

"Remember, you never heard of me or my friends," Thad reminded Patton.

McCallum nodded to Pedro, who led the way out the gate. The four rode up the hill to where the mules had been left. Fortunately, they found them grazing contentedly.

Lieutenant Patton took one last look at the bodies of the Mexicans, and then over at the cars. Patton grinned and pointed. "Sarge, have some of the men throw these four rebels over the hood of the lead car. Tie them down good."

"How's that, sir?" the sergeant asked.

"I'm going to strap these rebels to my car and then dump them at the general's tent flap. Yes, sir, by golly, that's exactly what we're going to do."

The sergeant had been in the Army long enough to know not to argue with an officer. He simply shrugged and shouted: "You heard the man! Strap 'em down and then let's get the hell outta here!"

Chapter Thirty-Five

McCallum, Pedro, Jeff, and Mercedes made it safely to Rubio, and from there they rode north until they could arrange transport on a train headed back to the border. When they arrived back in the good old U.S.A., all four breathed a sigh of relief.

The trip back had given McCallum time to reëvaluate the boy and his girl. Thad McCallum had always been hard to impress, but when he heard the whole story of how Jeff had survived and how he had won over such an obviously beautiful and independent girl as Mercedes Valdez de Guerrera his original opinion about him changed.

This was clearly no silly boy who had merely wandered into a hornet's nest as Thad had supposed. "Maybe there's more of Al in you than I thought," he had remarked to Jeff on the journey back to the States. Then, looking over at Mercedes, he had added: "One thing for sure, while you may have inherited some of his guts, you clearly got his charm and luck with the ladies."

Jeff was truly surprised at Thad's comments for two reasons. The first was that he had never thought of his father as being a ladies' man. Second, and more importantly, he had learned from Pedro that his godfather was a man of few words and had a reputation for seldom giving out compliments.

It was then that Thad told Jeff about his mother's illness.

"You know, when you bring a bride back with you, it might just make her happy and give her reason to keep on fighting to live. A mother likes to know her son is well cared for."

At this, Mercedes hugged Jeff tightly, wiping away the tear that had formed in his eye before she backed away.

By the time Pedro arranged train tickets home for Jeff and Mercedes, Thad had the pair outfitted with new clothes and the necessary travel gear. He had figured that if they wanted to start things out right when they got back to Jeff's family home, Mercedes couldn't arrive looking like a rebel with a pistol on her hip. Sure, Al might be amused, but Maggie was the one who counted. They would need her blessing. Looking at Mercedes, decked out in a new dress and Jeff in a suit with a stiff neck and tie, he felt sure they would receive it gladly.

As he stood there, Thad realized that he would miss the pair. He had few people in his life that he was close to, and hearing Jeff call him Uncle Thad had unexpectedly touched him. He liked the girl as well. She was spunky, independent, and strong. Those were characteristics McCallum admired in anyone. The fact that she was also beautiful was icing on the cake. He had actually blushed at the train station when she had given him a good-bye kiss.

Yep, he thought, *Al and Maggie will quickly fall in love with her, too. And maybe they'll return someday and bring along some grand-kids.*

As the train pulled out, Jeff and Mercedes leaned out the window and waved. Thad waved back and was deep in thought when Pedro suddenly slapped him on the back. "Time to mount up, *jefe*," he said as he took hold of the reins to their two horses. "What's that you always say . . . the day's a-wasting. First, we've got to let Jeff's uncle know everything is good. And we have horses to break back at the ranch. Right, *jefe*? Or should I say, Iron Sergeant?"

Thad McCallum glared angrily at his old friend, and then snarled: "If I didn't need your sorry ass back at the ranch so much, I'd tell you to go straight to hell."

The two looked at each other seriously for a moment, and then broke out into laughter. McCallum laughed so hard he couldn't catch his breath, which caused spasms of pain to pulse through his body. "Damned rheumatism," he hissed. He arched his stiff back and, before taking out his briar pipe, popped a couple of pieces of licorice in his mouth.

"*Vamanos*, you old horse thief," Thad said to his friend. "We got another long ride ahead of us."

Epilogue

Across the Río Bravo is a work of fiction, but like the rest of my novels there are elements of historical reality that come into play during the story.

There is a basis for the importance of photography in this tale. Pancho Villa was reputed to be a narcissistic man, and so the idea of promoting himself as a modernized Mexican version of "El Zorro" or perhaps a "Latin Robin Hood" would certainly have appealed to him. To that end, Villa participated in a film, part dramatization and part documentary footage of Villa's march and the battle of Torreon, entitled *The Life of General Villa*. It was released by Mutual Film Corporation in 1914. Although much of its making is clouded in misinformation, D.W. Griffith is credited variously as producer or supervisor while Christy Cabanne is credited as its director, as is Raoul Walsh for camera work on the newsreel footage for the battle scene in Torreon. Walsh also is said to have played the rôle of a young Villa in the dramatized section about his early life.

It is believed that Villa agreed to the filming because he needed the money for his fight in the revolution. (Some sources say he was paid the hefty sum of $25,000 for his participation.) It was thought that the film could make rich Americans sympathetic to the cause of Villa, who was the victim of evil landowners (*hacendados*) who had supposedly raped his sister and stolen his family's land and thus encourage donations to help his cause. Regardless, there is little doubt that Villa loved the idea of seeing himself recorded in photos and film to be saved for posterity.

General John Joseph (Black Jack) Pershing's Mexican Punitive Expedition is now considered a relatively unsuccessful venture by the United States. While the Army did eventually succeed in routing the revolutionary Army, it never did capture Pancho Villa.

Today the failure of the expedition is generally not considered to be Pershing's fault, but rather is attributed to the lack of co-operation from the Mexican government, the poor roads and primitive transportation, plus the break-down in the American Army's quartermaster corps.

When the United States did finally decide to enter World War One, Frederick Funston, Pershing's superior, was being considered to head the American Expeditionary Force. When General Funston died of a heart attack in February, 1917, Pershing was chosen to replace him and was eventually given the post of Commander of the American Expeditionary Force (AEF).

Black Jack's biggest contribution in the Great War is thought by many to be his absolute insistence that the American Army not be broken up and incorporated into French or English units, or fed into battle piecemeal. He insisted that the Army fight as an independent group and that he, as its commander, be given the respect due his post by our allies.

There is little doubt that the entrance of the American Army finally helped turn the tide of battle and win the war. Later, in 1919, as recognition of his distinguished service during World War I, the President promoted Pershing to the six-star rank of General of the Armies. He remains the only general in American military history ever to hold that rank while living. George Washington was granted that same high rank, but it was awarded posthumously in his case.

During his time as Chief of Staff of the Army, Pershing mentored many of the most famous generals to lead later on in the Second World War. Men such as Marshall, MacArthur, Eisenhower, and Patton were all influenced in one way or another by his command presence.

Pershing finally retired from active service in 1924. He remained highly visible in public life and at one point a movement to draft him as a Presidential candidate gained momentum, but Pershing declined to pursue the offer. General John J. (Black Jack) Pershing died on July 15, 1948.

George S. Patton, Jr., is now credited with leading what would become the first motorized attack in the history of U.S. warfare. His first real experience with combat occurred on May 14, 1916, when his men, driving three Dodge touring cars, surprised three of Villa's men during a foraging expedition.

During the resulting fire fight Julio Cardenas, one of Pancho Villa's captains, and two of his guards were killed. Patton later strapped their dead bodies over the hood of his car and dumped them at General Pershing's head-quarters. Because of Patton's actions, Black Jack Pershing would later refer to him affectionately as his *"Bandido"*.

After the fight at the San Miguelito Ranch, Patton carved two notches on his pistol grip. He would proudly carry that very same pistol on his hip all through the Second World War.

During the First World War Patton commanded the first tank school in France and was later wounded in combat. Between wars he became very close friends with another officer who was also interested in armored battle tactics, Dwight David Eisenhower. Together they would become America's top advocates for tank warfare.

General Patton's exploits in World War Two are legendary, and today his name is synonymous with bold, hard-driving tactics and personal bravery. Sadly, shortly after the war ended, Patton was involved in a tragic automobile accident that left him paralyzed. On December 21, 1945, four-star General George S. Patton, Jr., died as a result of his injuries.

Eventually his legendary fame rose to the extent that the movie, *Patton*, was release in 1970, about his war years. Starring George C. Scott as Patton, the film which won seven Oscars, remains an iconic classic.

Pancho Villa (1878-1923) was a Mexican bandit, warlord, and revolutionary. He was born José Doroteo Arango Arámbula on a small farm. It is hard to differentiate fact from fiction about his early life since Villa worked hard to create a new personal biography to fit his own needs.

It is claimed that at sixteen years of age Villa shot a man over an accusation of having accosted one of Villa's sisters. He was forced to flee and became a roving fugitive bandit.

Later Villa joined the rebel cause fighting to overthrow the current government. His fighting skills helped him to become one of the most important figures of the Mexican Revolution. Together with his famous *Division del Norte* he was instrumental in the downfall of two Mexican presidents: Porfirio Díaz and Victoriano Huerta.

Eventually Venustiano Carranza succeeded Huerta and began a governmental military campaign against Villa. By this time, Villa was viewed by most Mexican politicians as a rogue and a dangerously loose cannon. When his personal army, the *Division del Norte*, was eventually defeated by government troops, Villa was forced to resort to banditry to keep his remaining men supplied with food and ammunition. This in turn eventually led to his vicious attack on Columbus, New Mexico.

The Mexican Punitive Expedition was a ten-thousand men troop movement into Mexico tasked by the United States government with the job of eliminating the revolutionary army and capturing or killing Pancho Villa. It failed to do either, although for several months the revolutionary leader was forced into hiding while recuperating from battle wounds.

For the next several years Villa had to live as a recluse, hiding in the mountains. Even as hard as it tried, the Mexican government was completely unsuccessful in capturing this elusive rebel bandit. Eventually, in 1920, a deal was brokered with the current president of Mexico, Álvaro Obregón, to pardon Villa's actions and allow him to retire to a rather large *hacienda*.

Villa apparently lived quietly on his ranch and was at peace for a time, but four years later he was gunned down while driving his car through the town of Parral. Although it was never confirmed, the suspicion remains high that Obregón ordered the assassination over fears that Villa might be nominated as a presidential candidate in the 1924 elections.

Today most Mexicans have forgotten about Villa's cruel rôle in the blood bath that was the Revolution. They have, for the most part, forgotten his unjustified massacres, illegal executions, and assorted robberies. As far as the modern public is concerned what is left are stories of his daring and defiance. Thanks to many years of fictional Hollywood movies about him, Pancho Villa continues to be celebrated as a sort of latter day Mexican Robin Hood.

About the Author

R. W. Stone inherited his love for Western adventure from his father, a former Army Air Corps armaments officer and horse enthusiast. He taught his son both to ride and shoot at a very early age. Many of those who grew up in the late 1950s and early 1960s remember it as a time before urban sprawl when Westerns dominated both television and the cinema, and Stone began writing later in life in an attempt to recapture some of that past spirit he had enjoyed as a youth. In 1974 Stone graduated from the University of Illinois with honors in Animal Science. After living in Mexico for five years, he later graduated from the National Autonomous University's College of Veterinary Medicine and moved to Florida. Over the years he has served as President of the South Florida Veterinary Medical Association, the Lake County Veterinary Medical Association, and as executive secretary for three national veterinary organizations. Dr. Stone is currently the Chief of Staff of the Veterinary Trauma Center of Groveland, an advanced level care facility. In addition to lecturing internationally, he is the author of over seventy scientific articles and a number of Westerns, including *Trail Hand* (2006). Still a firearms collector, horse enthusiast, and now a black-belt-ranked martial artist, R. W. Stone presently lives in Central Florida with his wife, two daughters, one horse, and three dogs.

Books are produced
in the United States
using U.S.-based
materials

Books are printed
using a revolutionary
new process called
THINKtech™ that
lowers energy usage
by 70% and increases
overall quality

Books are durable
and flexible because
of smythe-sewing

Paper is sourced
using environmentally
responsible foresting
methods and the
paper is acid-free

Center Point Large Print
600 Brooks Road / PO Box 1
Thorndike, ME 04986-0001 USA

(207) 568-3717

US & Canada:
1 800 929-9108
www.centerpointlargeprint.com